GRAVENHUNGER

TO NICK...

...AND TO JOEL BEARN
OF VERNON PRIMARY
SCHOOL, POYNTON

STRIPES PUBLISHING
An imprint of Little Tiger Press
1 The Coda Centre, 189 Munster Road
London SW6 6AW

A paperback original
First published in Great Britain in 2011

Text copyright © Harriet Goodwin, 2011
Cover copyright © Stripes Publishing Ltd, 2011
Original house image copyright © iStockphoto.com, 2011
Inside illustrations copyright © Richard Allen, 2011

ISBN 978-1-84715-154-4

Printed and bound in the UK by CPI Group (UK) Ltd, Croydon, CR0 4YY

10 9 8 7 6 5 4 3

GRAVENHUNGER

Stripes

Harriet Goodwin

1.
ELVIRA'S LETTER

"No way!" said Phoenix, glaring at his father across the kitchen table. "I'm not going. Not for the whole of the summer holidays. And not with *Rose!*"

Dr Wainwright sighed. He put down his knife and fork and leaned back in his chair.

"What's wrong with Rose? She was nice enough to you at the funeral, wasn't she?"

Phoenix dropped his gaze.

"Of course she was nice to me at the funeral," he muttered. "Everyone was. But that doesn't mean I want to go on holiday with her! Six weeks, Dad! With a girl I hardly know! What on earth were you thinking?"

"I was partly thinking of your cousin, actually," said Dr Wainwright.

He ran his fingers through his greying hair.

"Rose has just come back from four years abroad. I don't suppose she's made many friends at her new school yet, so I thought she might like to come on holiday with us."

Phoenix scowled.

"But why couldn't I have asked one of my mates from school? Jake or Sam, maybe?" He pushed his plate to one side. "And what's with all this going away business, anyway? We never go on holiday. Never. Why change things now? And why spring it on me at the last minute?"

His father raised his eyebrows. "Because I knew you'd kick up one almighty great fuss," he said. "Exactly like you're doing now."

Phoenix flushed and fumbled in his pocket for a piece of chewing gum.

"Look," his father went on. "You're right, we never go on holiday. You know Mum couldn't stand being away from home. But – well, things are different now. And I thought a proper break would do us good." He glanced at his son's pale face. "Goodness knows we could do with one after the year we've had."

There was a long silence.

"So what's this place like, anyway?" said Phoenix at last. "What did you say it was called again?"

"Gravenhunger Manor. It's on the south coast. A couple of miles outside the village of Gravenhunger."

Phoenix rolled his eyes.

"Honestly, Dad. First holiday we've ever been on and you go and choose some old place by the sea I've never even heard of. Why couldn't we have gone abroad? Why couldn't we have gone somewhere *interesting*?"

"You know we can't afford that sort of holiday," replied his father. "Especially since the university cut back on my teaching hours. Things aren't easy at the moment, Phoenix. Besides, I think you'll like where we're going. Gravenhunger Manor must have been very grand in its day. The house is huge and so are the grounds. There's a big garden at the back and a pine forest surrounding the whole thing, and a river beyond the trees. It's got something about it. Something unusual. Something different."

"Yeah?" said Phoenix. "And how would you know that?" He frowned suddenly. "You've been there before, haven't you?"

Dr Wainwright shifted in his seat. He opened his mouth to speak, then shut it again.

Phoenix folded his arms, his eyes now fixed upon his father.

"Come on, Dad. There's something you're not telling me, isn't there?"

9

His father cleared his throat. "There *is* something I need to tell you about Gravenhunger Manor. But…"

"But what?"

"It's a bit tricky, that's all. I was going to leave it till we were on our way down there tomorrow. I thought the journey would give us a chance for a good long chat before Rose arrives."

"Can't you tell me now?"

"The last thing I want to do is stir things up for you, Phoenix…"

"Dad! Stop treating me like a little kid! I'm nearly thirteen, in case you'd forgotten."

Dr Wainwright rested his elbows on the table and met his son's gaze.

"All right," he said. "You win. I'll tell you what all this is about."

He took off his glasses and rubbed his eyes.

"This place we're going to," he said, "this house in the middle of nowhere. It – it belonged to your mother. Gravenhunger Manor belonged to her."

"To *Mum*?"

Phoenix gaped at his father.

"But she never said anything. She never even mentioned it."

"No, not to you – and not to me either."

"You're saying you didn't know anything about it?"

Dr Wainwright replaced his glasses and shook his head. "Nothing at all," he said. "Not until the solicitor's papers landed on my desk back in February. It was just as much a surprise to me then as it is to you now."

"But *why* didn't she say anything? Did she leave you some sort of an explanation?"

His father glanced away. He picked up his fork and began to push his unfinished food around the plate.

"Not really," he said. "All I know is that Gravenhunger Manor was bought by your mother's parents many years ago. It seems they lived there for a short time when your mum was a child. For whatever reason the house was never sold when they moved on – so when your grandparents died, it was passed down to your mother."

"And now it's yours?"

"That's right. Which is why I thought it'd be a good idea to go down there this summer and take a proper look at it."

"But I still don't understand," said Phoenix. "Why would Mum keep something like that secret?"

Dr Wainwright got up from the table. "I'm afraid it's all a bit of a mystery," he said, gathering up the plates and carrying them over to the worktop. "But I expect she had her reasons."

He stood there for a moment, his back to his son. "Your mother was quite a complicated person, you know."

"And what's that supposed to mean?" demanded Phoenix.

His father turned round to face him. "Don't get me wrong," he said. "She was a wonderful mother and she loved you with all her heart. But she was a woman of secrets. She always held herself back. Not so much from you, perhaps. But certainly from me."

A shadow passed across his face.

"Just think about how long she kept her illness from us both. She knew how to keep things quiet. And it looks like it was the same with this house. If she had some reason not to tell us about it, then we just have to respect that. I'm not about to start raking things up. There's no point. We have to look forward now, you and I. Find a way to start again."

Phoenix looked away.

A woman of secrets. It was weird hearing Dad talk about Mum like that. It didn't seem right.

He pictured the little silver angel, zipped inside his blazer pocket upstairs.

That had been a sort of secret too, now he came to think about it. But at least it was one Mum had chosen to share with him.

She had given him the angel the day before she

died. He'd never seen it before, but it clearly meant the world to her. She'd put it into his hands, her dark eyes searching his face, and asked him to keep it safe.

And so he had taken it, fighting back the tears and trying not to look too hard at the grey face on the pillow before him. Since that day he had carried it with him everywhere, knowing neither how nor why it soothed him, knowing only that it was his special link with her, and that he couldn't be without it. It wasn't exactly cool to own an angel, but he was never going to let it go.

Phoenix picked up the chewing-gum wrapper from the table and started to tear it into minute shreds.

"So anyway, you've been down there, have you?" he muttered. "To this Gravenhunger Manor?"

"Just the once," replied his father. "A week or so after I received the news from the solicitor. I thought I should check it out. See what kind of state it was in. After all, it hasn't been lived in for thirty years."

He came back over to the table and sat down.

"When your mother's family left there, a trust fund was set up to look after it. It paid for a local woman to come in once in a while and keep things ticking over. But the fund dried up a year or so ago, and the lady from the village was getting too old to look after it anyway, so by the time I visited, no one had actually set foot in the place for over a year."

"And what was it like?" asked Phoenix.

His father shrugged.

"Huge entrance hall, masses of rooms, lots of garden – quite the stately home…"

"No, Dad, what was it *really* like?"

Dr Wainwright sighed. "To be honest it was pretty dismal. It poured with rain the whole time I was there, which didn't exactly help. I only stayed a few hours. Just long enough to have a bit of a tidy and board up a couple of broken windows."

He looked at Phoenix, his expression brightening.

"But it was February when I went down, remember. Not exactly the time to bring out the best in anywhere. I'm sure it'll feel completely different now. It's summer, after all. And we're in for a heatwave, by all accounts. I thought we could take the bikes down with us. If you use mine, I'm sure Rose can manage with yours."

The sound of the telephone made them both jump.

Phoenix stayed at the table while his father crossed to the hallway to answer it.

A couple of minutes later he was back.

"That was Mrs Hopwood. She's going to keep an eye on our house while we're away and I need to drop the spare keys round."

He picked up his jacket and slung it over his shoulder.

"I won't be long. Why don't you go upstairs and make a start on your packing? I'd like to get off as early as possible tomorrow morning. Beat the worst of the holiday traffic."

Phoenix said nothing. He waited until the front door latch had clicked back into place, then got to his feet and slumped out of the kitchen.

In the hallway he stopped.

The door to his father's study stood slightly ajar.

He hesitated.

The last time he'd gone in there he'd landed himself in big trouble. He'd been hunting for a school trip consent form which had needed signing, and had accidentally moved some papers around on the desk. Not exactly a crime punishable by death. But Dad had gone ballistic. Told him he'd messed up the order of his precious scientific documents.

Phoenix sighed at the memory.

Quite what his father meant by order he had no idea. Every square inch of his desk was covered in folders and books and tiny scraps of paper. How Dad knew where to find anything was completely beyond him.

Even so, he'd learned his lesson. He'd set about teaching himself how to forge his father's signature on school letters and vowed never to set foot in the study again.

Now, though, he wasn't so sure he could keep that promise.

Dad hadn't been entirely honest with him back there in the kitchen, he could have sworn it. All that shifting around, the messing about with his food, the failure to meet his eye.

When he'd asked whether Mum had left some kind of explanation for keeping this house of hers secret, he hadn't really given a straight answer, had he? What if he was being sparing with the truth? What if he knew more than he was letting on? And if so, might there be something lying around that might just help him understand all this? Something it was his *right* to know about?

Phoenix pursed his lips.

He glanced out of the hallway window to where his father was being ushered into the next-door neighbour's house…

…and then he pushed open the study door.

From between the half-pulled curtains a shaft of sunlight shone into the study, illuminating a long cone of floating dust particles.

Phoenix stared around him. It was a warm-looking room, strewn with rugs in reds and blues and creams and full of the musty smell of old books.

Down one wall was a row of bookshelves, sagging under the weight of their contents, and at the far end, just to one side of the window, stood his father's war-zone of a desk.

It had been Dad's bolthole ever since Phoenix could remember. Even as a little boy, on his way to find his mother in the kitchen, he had taken care to lighten his step as he had passed by, aware of the important scientific work being done inside.

Recently, though, his father seemed to have been spending more time in it than ever.

Perhaps it was just his way of coping, but since Mum had died, he had practically lived in his study, emerging at mealtimes only to remember that if he wanted food then he would have to get it himself.

And so he would fix the pair of them a sandwich or order some tasteless food from the takeaway down the road and they would sit there in silence while they ate. Then he would slope back off to his study, leaving Phoenix to clear up, alone with his mixed-up feelings and the fragile memories of his mother.

Which made whatever it was that was going on right now seem weirder than ever. This evening Dad had actually cooked a meal for them. Made it from scratch with real, fresh ingredients, chopping the vegetables and frying the onions and boiling up the rice.

Of course it was possible the whole thing had been one big softening-up exercise. That it had all been done in preparation for springing the news of this surprise trip on him.

Phoenix crossed the room to his father's desk.

Standing in amongst the books and bits of paper and half-empty coffee mugs was a silver photo frame, its back towards him.

He picked it up and turned it round, a sharp and now familiar pain piercing his chest as he took in the picture of himself and his mother.

It had been taken only a few months before she died. They were sitting together on the garden seat, her arm draped loosely round his shoulders, so alike it was almost uncanny: the same jet-black hair, the same dark eyes, the same firm set of the chin.

He hadn't known she was ill back then. He hadn't even had the faintest clue. He could see it now, though. The strain in her face and the paleness of her skin. And she was thin too. Really thin. How had he failed to notice?

He could still remember the warmth of her touch ... how she had stooped to kiss him every night ... the musky scent of her perfume. Tucked away in the bottom of his chest of drawers he had one of her old scarves, and when he couldn't sleep he would sometimes take it into bed with him and press it to his face, desperate to inhale some of its fading sweetness.

Phoenix sighed. He missed her so much.

It wasn't that they'd done particularly exciting things together or anything like that. Mum hadn't been that sort of person. What Dad had said at dinner had been quite true. She'd hated the idea of being away from home, which meant they'd never once gone on holiday like other people's families did.

But it had never really mattered. Mum had made up for it in other ways.

There were the little messages she used to leave him in his lunch box when he was younger. Scraps of paper hidden amongst the foil packages, telling him what she had planned for the weekend or what she was cooking for dinner. Of course, if his friends ever spotted them he would pretend they meant nothing and slam the lid back on, but secretly he'd loved finding them in there.

And then there were all the conversations they had shared. Conversations over the breakfast table; conversations on the way to school; conversations last thing at night before he went to bed. He had never held back, chattering away nineteen to the dozen about anything and everything, loving the way she listened to him so intently, the way she seemed to know him inside out.

Phoenix swallowed.

He put down the photo frame and scanned the papers strewn across the top of the desk – then went round to the drawers at the front.

It was possible, of course, that something might have been tucked inside one of the hundreds of dusty old academic books that lined the shelves. But sifting through those would take for ever. He would just have to make do with a quick look through the desk.

For a fraction of a second he paused, his hands halfway to the top drawer.

He would kill anyone who did this to him: rummaging through his personal possessions without his permission.

But the lure of what he might find inside overpowered his guilt – and besides, if they were making an early start in the morning, it was now or never.

Phoenix pulled open the drawer.

There was hardly anything inside it – just a box of paper clips and some stationery.

And there was nothing much in the next one down either.

Perhaps his instincts had been wrong after all.

Perhaps Dad really did know nothing more about Mum's reasons for keeping the house secret than he had told him at the dinner table.

He crouched down to open the bottom drawer of the desk, then frowned.

Inside it was a red folder. Quite a new one by the look of it, the price label still attached.

Phoenix lifted it out, and there, written in large capital letters in the top right-hand corner, were the two words he had been hoping to find ... GRAVENHUNGER MANOR.

Something hard and heavy was lying at the bottom of the folder – and sliding his hand into it, he drew out a huge, old-fashioned brass key.

For a moment he held the key in the palm of his hand, marvelling at the sheer weight of it, wondering at the size of the lock it would open. And then he dropped it back into the folder and began sifting through the papers that had been filed inside.

At the front was a formal-looking document with his mother's signature on it, and behind that were a few other pieces of paper, including an ancient electricity bill and some stuff from the council.

But that was it.

Nothing that looked even remotely interesting.

Sighing, he made to replace the folder – then stopped, his eye caught by a tiny flash of gold at the back of the drawer. Something had been pinned to the wood: a cream-coloured envelope held in position by a single drawing pin.

He put down the folder and unfastened the envelope from its hiding place…

…and there it was, in faded black ink – his father's name laced across the centre in his mother's handwriting, calling to him from another world.

Phoenix jumped as the carriage clock on the mantelpiece chimed the hour. Dad would be back soon. Even Mrs Hopwood with her chatterbox ways couldn't keep him talking much longer.

If he was going to do this, he didn't have long.

Quickly, he lifted the flap and pulled out a single sheet of paper, his guts twisting at the sight of the same spidery hand that had looped his father's name on the front of the envelope. Straightening up, he smoothed it out and began to read.

My dearest Joel,

By now you will have received the news that you have inherited Gravenhunger Manor.

I'm sorry you have had to find out about it this way – that I didn't have the courage to tell you in my last weeks. I expect it has all come as a bit of a shock.

But telling you about it myself would have led to questions. Questions which, after all this time, I do not think I could have found it in myself to answer.

I owe you, however, at least some kind of explanation. Please accept this as the best I can give.

My parents moved to Gravenhunger Manor when I was twelve years old. They had grown tired of city life, so when my father was offered a job near the coast, it seemed their prayers had been answered, and together they ploughed their savings into the purchase of what was to become our new home.

It was the most magical place I had ever set eyes on. I could see the blue sea from my bedroom window and the river running at the bottom of the pine forest. It was a child's paradise.

But something happened there, Joel. Something so terrible that we left only a few weeks after we arrived.

From outside, Phoenix could hear voices drifting on the evening air. He edged towards the window and glanced out, taking care to keep behind the curtains.

His father was standing on the neighbour's doorstep, nodding and smiling and saying his goodbyes.

He flicked his gaze back to the letter.

Exactly what happened is a secret. No one ever knew the truth but me – not even my poor, dear parents. It is a secret I have chosen to take with me to the grave. Know only that it was every bit my fault – and that I will never forgive myself, neither in this life nor in the life to come.

After we left, my parents tried to sell Gravenhunger Manor, but nobody would buy it. When they died, the house was passed down to me in their will. I did not try to sell it. It was easier simply to keep away.

Footsteps were coming up the garden path…

Sell the place if you wish, Joel. Use the money to make you both comfortable. Nothing would give me greater pleasure.

Take good care of yourself – and above all, look after Phoenix. He is your very greatest treasure.

Your loving wife,

Elvira

His hands shaking, Phoenix tucked the letter inside the envelope again. He bent to re-pin it to the back of the drawer and replaced the folder as he'd found it.

Then he slid the desk drawer shut and hurried out into the hallway – just as his father pushed open the front door.

2.
GRAVENHUNGER
MANOR

Phoenix blinked back the sunlight that was streaming towards him and looked at the clock on the dashboard.

Only eleven o'clock, and even with all the windows open the car was like an oven. Perhaps they really were in for a heatwave this summer. It certainly felt that way.

"You've been spark out for nearly two hours," said his father, glancing across at him. "Didn't you get much sleep last night?" He swung the car down a narrow lane bordered by low hedges and clumps of yellow gorse. "Were you thinking about what I told you last night? About your mum and Gravenhunger Manor, I mean? D'you want to talk about it?"

Phoenix shook his head. "No thanks, Dad. It's cool, OK."

His father raised his eyebrows. "Are you sure? It must have been a bit of a shock."

A bit of a shock. It was the same expression his mother had used in her letter. *I'm sorry you have had to find out about it this way ... I expect it has all come as a bit of a shock.*

Too right it was a shock. How else were you supposed to feel when the person you thought you knew so well, the person you had shared all your thoughts and worries and feelings with, turned out to have had a strange and secret past?

"Really, Dad, I'm fine," he murmured. "I'm tired after the school term, that's all. In any case, it's too hot to talk about anything right now."

He closed his eyes again and turned away.

It wasn't that he blamed Dad for keeping quiet about the letter. After all, he must have been feeling pretty mixed-up about the whole thing himself. It was just that what he had read was completely doing his head in, and the last thing he wanted to do was talk about it.

He had lain awake for hours last night, going over and over his mother's mysterious words in his mind.

...something happened there ... something so terrible that we left only a few weeks after we arrived ... it was every bit my fault ... I will never forgive myself, neither in this life nor in the life to come.

What on earth was this terrible thing that had caused the family to leave Gravenhunger Manor in such a hurry? And why hadn't she felt able to share whatever it was with him and Dad?

When sleep had come at last, he had been swept up into a wild tangle of dreams, where image after image of his mother had flashed before him. Images of her reading to him when he was a small child; images of her face the day she had told them she was ill; images of her right at the very end.

He had woken drenched in sweat, his stomach churning, waiting for dawn to rescue him from the suffocating darkness.

Phoenix shifted in his seat, relaxing a little as he felt the silver angel nudge against his leg from inside his jeans pocket.

One thing was certain. He was going to use every second of his time at Gravenhunger Manor to find out what had happened there all those years ago. Exactly how he would go about it he didn't yet know, but he wouldn't rest until he had uncovered the truth.

Beside him, his father's voice roused him from his thoughts.

"Nearly there now," he was saying. "I caught a glimpse of the sea just then. It's such a wonderfully clear day."

He checked the clock.

"There should be just enough time to open up the house and get the bags in before I need to collect Rose from her train."

Phoenix groaned to himself.

If only Dad hadn't invited his cousin to stay with them. Having her around was going to make finding things out a million times more difficult.

He glanced outside as the car slowed to a halt beside a narrow track leading off through a forest of pines. A pair of rusty entrance gates, long since fallen from their hinges, lay in the undergrowth, half covered in drifts of pine needles.

He screwed up his eyes in an effort to read the signpost that stood at the side of the road. But where words had once been, only the ghost of letters remained – and he could only guess at what must lie at the end of the track that snaked its way through the forest and out of sight.

Rose stepped off the train into the stream of passengers heading towards the main station concourse.

She was practically dying of heat.

The onboard trolley service had run out of drinks halfway through the journey and then the air conditioning had broken down in her carriage, sending the temperature rocketing, along with everybody's tempers.

But she was here at last, and with half an hour to spare before her connection left for the coast, at least now she could get a drink and find somewhere to cool off.

It seemed like only yesterday since the journey back from Dad's last posting abroad, and here she was on the move again, after less than a month of getting used to life at home, all set to spend the entire holidays in some weird old house by the sea with her cousin and uncle.

Even now she could hardly believe she had let her parents talk her into it.

Still, it wasn't as if she'd had any better offers. They weren't going away as a family this summer, and although she was beginning to make friends at her new school, no one was about to invite her to go on holiday with them, were they? In any case, Mum reckoned her cousin was lonely and needed a bit of company. He'd certainly looked pretty terrible at the funeral, his face all pinched and tight, his eyes ringed with dark circles. She'd tried talking to him after the service, but he'd barely said a word – just bent his head and stabbed at the frosty January ground with his shoe. In the end she'd given up and gone off to talk to somebody else.

Rose dumped her rucksack outside the newsagent's. She pushed a stray red curl from her face, then reached into one of the side pockets for her purse.

Phoenix, her cousin was called – after his mother's maiden name, apparently.

Fancy giving your kid a name like that. What on earth had Uncle Joel and Aunt Elvira been thinking? She sighed.

It had been years since she had seen her aunt, yet she remembered her quite clearly. A tall, slim woman with eyes so dark they were nearly black, her raven hair cropped like a boy's. Half Italian, Mum said. Apparently Uncle Joel had fallen for her at first sight.

Something had stopped her from being truly beautiful though: the too-deep creases in her forehead, perhaps – or the sad look in her eyes. It was as if someone had come along and sucked the fun out of her.

Rose shuddered. Just the thought of losing one of her parents was too much to bear. Poor Phoenix. She would do everything she possibly could to cheer him up.

Hitching her rucksack back on to one shoulder, she stepped inside the newsagent's.

She took a bottle of water from the cooler and made her way towards the counter, cursing under her breath as the corner of her rucksack caught against a shelf of maps and guidebooks, knocking a pale blue booklet to the floor.

A Guide to Gravenhunger, she read, bending to pick up the little volume. There was a photo of a busy harbour on the front cover, and on the back a shot of what was almost certainly the high street, all brightly coloured shops and stripy awnings.

Glancing at the booklet, she considered for a moment, then tucked it under her arm and joined the queue at the counter.

It was probably only a collection of dry old facts, not worth the paper it was written on, but she would buy it anyway.

It would help pass the time for the rest of the journey.

The car rattled over the ruts and potholes, scattering rabbits in every direction.

Everywhere was thick with brambles, their spiky tendrils reaching across the track as if trying to knit together the two sides of the forest. But for the occasional snatch of sky, it seemed they had been swallowed up in a never-ending tunnel of deep and shadowy green.

Now they were veering off to the right and something else was coming into view.

Phoenix gasped.

How could she have kept a place like this a secret?

It was huge. Four storeys of dark grey stone glowering down at them through a multitude of mullioned windows. Ivy trailed from the rooftops and over the gigantic front door there hung an ancient hurricane lamp, its glass casing cracked and blackened.

He shivered as a gust of wind blew in through the car window and caught the hairs on the back of his neck.

The sun had disappeared behind a dense bank of cloud – and above the towering chimneys of Gravenhunger Manor a thin grey rain was falling.

If any more daytrippers tried to squeeze on to the train, Rose reckoned it would never move out of the station.

Gravenhunger was obviously a very popular seaside resort, and she didn't need to read her guidebook to prove it.

Her own carriage was full of families mainly: pink-faced women clutching even pinker-faced babies on their knees while their husbands bribed older children with sweets and crisps. There were teenagers too, blowing bubble gum and listening to music and texting on their mobiles.

She could imagine them all now, spilling out into the hot July sunshine at the other end of the line, in search of sun and sand and sea and freedom.

At least the air conditioning was working on this train. And at least she had a seat, even if it did happen to be next to an old man in a tweed cap who seemed intent on peering over her shoulder at her guidebook.

She couldn't help feeling just the tiniest bit proud of herself. OK, so she'd done long train journeys alone before, but she'd never had to change from one train to another.

Mum had been in two minds as to whether to let her do it at all, but Dad had talked her into it, reasoning that their daughter was more than up to the challenge and that it would be a character-building experience.

That was Dad all over. Always eager to drag her and Mum off on some crazy adventure or other. Sometimes she wished he'd just ease off a bit.

From outside the carriage the guard blew his whistle and the train jolted into action.

Beside her, the old man lurched forward in his seat, then subsided into a raucous fit of coughing.

Rose edged towards the window, trying not to breathe in the heavy fumes of whisky and tobacco that were now wafting her way.

It was going to be a long journey.

"I can't do it," muttered Phoenix, wiping the rain from his face and jiggling the key in the lock. "It just won't open."

His father lifted the bikes down from the roofrack and leaned them up against the wall of the manor. Then he brought the bags over to the front door and held out his hand for the key.

"Let me try," he said. "It was like this when I came down before. It took me for ever to get in."

He pushed the key into the lock and turned it to the right, then jerked the old brass handle towards him.

The door shuddered open at last, creaking on its hinges, and a damp chill seeped across the threshold to greet them.

Ahead lay a vast entrance hall, bigger than any room Phoenix had ever set eyes on.

It was as unwelcoming as it was huge, its walls dark with damp, its paintwork peeling, its flagstoned floor bare and uncarpeted. In the centre a wooden staircase spiralled up and away out of sight and in one corner a grandfather clock glared down at them, its unmoving hands stuck at twenty minutes to four.

Dr Wainwright heaved their luggage in from the rain and glanced at his watch.

"I'm going to have to leave you to it, I'm afraid,"

he said. "I don't want Rose waiting at the station. Why don't you choose yourself a room and make up the bed? The sheets and pillowcases are in that bag there."

Phoenix nodded. "Dad?"

"Yes?"

"Does Rose know about all this? About the house having belonged to Mum, I mean?"

Dr Wainwright shook his head. "No. I had to explain things to her parents, of course, but I asked them to keep it to themselves. I thought we could tell her once she was here – after you'd had a chance to get used to the idea."

"Can't we just not tell her at all?" asked Phoenix. "I mean, it's our business, isn't it, not anybody else's?"

His father gave a small smile.

"I think we'll have to tell her sooner rather than later. I mean, this isn't exactly your usual holiday accommodation, is it? But I'm sure we can keep things vague for the moment, especially if you feel so strongly about it." He turned towards the door. "I'll pick up some essentials on the way back. Matches and firelighters for a start. It looks like we might be needing them later on. Goodness only knows what's happened to the weather."

Halfway to the car he stopped.

"You'll stay near the house, won't you?" he called

back through the rain. "The grounds are pretty wild to say the least. We can have a bit of an explore tomorrow, perhaps. But I don't want you going beyond the garden without me, OK?"

Phoenix rolled his eyes. "I can look after myself, you know. I told you, I'm not a kid any more."

His father sighed.

"I'm well aware of that," he replied. "But you're still my son."

He hurried on towards the car and opened the door before turning round once again.

"And you're all I've got."

Phoenix flushed.

He stared down at the grey stone floor, listening as the car revved up and crunched across the gravelled driveway.

Only when he was sure he was quite alone did he make his way across the hallway, his footsteps echoing on the flagstones.

He stopped at the foot of the staircase and looked up into the eerie gloom.

The bed-making business could wait till later. Somewhere up there was his mother's old room – the room from which she had gazed out at the sea and the river and the pine forest – and before he did anything else, he was going to find it.

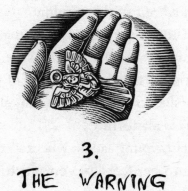

3.
THE WARNING

He was doing it again. Craning over her shoulder and wheezing with the effort of reading the text in the far corner of the page. It was really starting to get on her nerves.

Rose gave the old man a sidelong glance and snapped the guidebook shut.

If he wanted to read *A Guide to Gravenhunger* then he could go and buy a copy for himself. She was sick to death of sharing hers.

Not that it was proving exactly fascinating reading: so far it seemed to be just one long list of attractions. What to do on the pier; what to do in the arcades along the seafront; where to go and what to do in the town itself. She would have been much better off buying a magazine instead.

Rose looked out of the window.

They had to be very nearly there: gulls wheeled overhead and towards the horizon she could make out the occasional tantalizing sparkle of sea.

And now she could see something else too – the end of a station platform…

"Not so fast, young lady!" wheezed the old man, as she sprang to her feet. "No one's getting out here. We go straight through this one."

Sure enough the train was rattling past the platform edge, too quickly for Rose to read the name on the signs, too quickly for her to notice anything much more than a station overgrown with weeds.

For a couple of seconds they were engulfed in a blur of brambles and bindweed and peeling paint.

And then it was behind them, and they were rushing onward between rows of pastel-coloured seaside houses towards their destination.

It was almost as if the little station had not existed.

"Gravenhunger Reach," declared the old man solemnly as Rose sat back down. "There's not been a train pulled up there in years. No need for it, you see. Not now there's nobody living at the house."

"What house?" asked Rose, turning to meet the old man's gaze.

His face was brown and crinkled like a walnut, his mouth puckered up and thin, but his eyes were sharp enough, bright as pins and the colour of forget-me-nots.

"Gravenhunger Manor," he replied. "The big house on the other side of the river. No one's lived there for years and years."

"But that's where I'm going," said Rose. "It's where I'm staying this summer."

The old man gaped at her, revealing a mouthful of crooked yellow teeth.

"But you can't be!" he exclaimed. "Gravenhunger Manor's all packed up and empty."

"I guess someone must have opened it back up," said Rose, shrugging.

The old man muttered something under his breath, then gave way to another bout of coughing.

"It's well known in the area, is it, this Gravenhunger Manor?" asked Rose, when he had recovered himself.

"I should say so," said the old man. "Round here *everyone's* heard of it. There's that many stories about the place."

He leaned forward, his face now so close to Rose she could feel the warmth of his whisky breath on her skin.

"You want to take good care of yourself, young lady. There's some say Gravenhunger Manor's haunted."

Rose suppressed a laugh.

"Right," she said. "I'll – er – bear that in mind."
She cleared her throat. "And you say no one's lived
there for some time?"

"Not for over thirty years," said the old man. "Not
since…"

But whatever he was about to say was drowned
out by an announcement that they were arriving at
Gravenhunger, and by the time Rose had heaved her
rucksack down from the luggage rack and settled it
on to her back, she had been caught up in the sea of
passengers preparing to leave the train, and the old
man had disappeared.

Fighting her way down the aisle, Rose reached the
train doors at last and stepped out on to the sun-
drenched platform.

In the distance she could see her uncle waving at
her from the ticket barrier.

She waved back, smiling.

This was the moment she had been waiting for all
day: a light sea breeze ruffled her hair and she could
taste the tang of salt on her lips.

Halfway along the platform she felt a hand on her
shoulder. Spinning round, she came face to face with
the old man.

"Just you remember what I said," he hissed. "It's a
funny old place, Gravenhunger Manor. Strange things
happen there, you mark my words."

He fixed her with his forget-me-not eyes.

"Don't go wandering off on your own, that's my advice. And whatever you do, keep away from the mound on the other side of the river."

Rose blinked at him, then turned and headed on towards the station exit.

Really, there was no stopping some people's imaginations.

On the fourth-floor landing Phoenix paused.

Something here just wasn't adding up.

I could see the blue sea from my bedroom window – those were the words his mother had used in her letter. *I could see the blue sea from my bedroom window and the river running at the bottom of the pine forest.*

Well, he'd lost count of the number of windows he'd looked through – there had to be at least six or seven bedrooms on each floor – and all he'd seen through the rain was the forest on every side of the house and the overgrown garden at the back. There had been no sign of any river however hard he had strained his eyes, and not even the faintest glimpse of sea.

He could have sworn he'd seen only four storeys when he'd looked up at the manor from outside earlier on. But was it possible there was another floor, a room higher up that he'd somehow missed?

Phoenix scoured the wall in front of him.

There was a bookcase packed with dusty volumes … a portrait of a young woman dressed in green velvet … a threadbare tapestry…

And then he saw it, half concealed behind the tapestry: a small, brass doorknob.

He hesitated for a moment, his hand on the doorknob, then gave it a sharp twist and pulled open an oak-panelled door.

A dark stairwell stretched before him, its narrow steps spiralling up and out of sight.

Phoenix began to climb, wincing at the creak of ancient floorboards beneath his feet.

One … two … three…

Four … five … six…

He steadied himself against the stairway walls.

Seven … eight…

Ahead of him was another door.

Phoenix reached out and turned the handle.

There was a groan of wood and the door swung open to reveal a low-beamed attic room, furnished with a bed and a chest of drawers.

It was smaller than the other rooms – more of a garret, really.

And there was something else different about it too.

Even through the rain he could see it, sparkling in a distant patch of sunlight like a treasure trove of jewels. The promised view of the sea — and much closer, the occasional flash of river as it wove its way seaward past the pine trees.

Phoenix let out a long sigh.

So this had been his mother's bedroom. Only for a few weeks, maybe. Only until the terrible secret thing, whatever it was, had driven her family from the house for ever. But this room he was standing in right now had belonged to her.

Fumbling inside his pocket, he drew out the silver angel and nestled it in the palm of his hand.

He stroked his thumb over its wings, the sculpted metal rough and hard against his skin.

Had she had it then, he wondered — a little brighter perhaps, a bit less scratched and tarnished, but the same nevertheless?

Phoenix folded his fingers around his mother's keepsake and squeezed it tightly, then slid it back into his pocket and crossed to the window.

Something had caught his eye — something rising up between the river and the sea, set all on its own in the middle of a stretch of land and wreathed in ribbons of swirling mist...

...a vast, barrow-shaped mound.

4.
THE VIEW FROM
THE ATTIC

Dr Wainwright shouldered his niece's rucksack and led the way out towards the station car park.

"It's wonderful to see you, Rose," he said. "Really it is. I can't tell you how pleased I am you're here. And I see you've been making friends already!"

He nodded back to where the old man was showing his ticket at the barrier.

Rose grinned. "I sat next to him on the way down. He was winding me up with stories about Gravenhunger Manor."

Her uncle raised his eyebrows.

"Stories?" he asked, stopping beside the car and unlocking it. "What kind of stories?"

He stowed the rucksack in the boot and opened the passenger door for his niece to get in.

"Oh, you know the kind of thing," replied Rose. "Hauntings. Strange goings-on. That sort of rubbish."

Dr Wainwright laughed. "The place certainly has character, I'll give it that. Bucketloads of it. But as far as hauntings go, I really don't think you've got anything to worry about on that score!"

Rose settled back in the car and wiped the sweat from her forehead.

"So how did you get to hear about it, anyway?" she asked, as her uncle climbed into the driver's seat beside her. "Mum and Dad didn't seem to know much. And the old man on the train seemed quite surprised when I told him I was staying there. He said it hadn't been lived in for ages."

"Well, he was right about that at least," said her uncle, starting the engine and pulling out of the car park. "No one's lived at Gravenhunger Manor for thirty years." He cleared his throat. "Actually, Rose, I don't know much about the place. We kind of agreed to look after it for someone during the summer, you see. But don't worry, it's not in such a bad state. It just needs a good airing."

Rose smiled. "I'm sure it'll be great, Uncle Joel. Where's Phoenix, by the way?"

"I left him at the house," said Dr Wainwright. "He's supposed to be unpacking, but I expect he'll be out exploring. We need to stop off for a couple of things in the village and then we can head straight back and find him. I'm sure he'll be pleased to see you."

"I doubt it," said Rose. "We hardly know each other, really. To be honest I'm surprised he wanted me here at all."

"Don't be ridiculous," replied her uncle. "You'll be a breath of fresh air. Exactly what he needs. Exactly what *both* of us need."

Rose blushed to the roots of her red hair.

"So what are we stopping off for?" she asked, keen to change the subject. "Food for tonight?"

Her uncle turned the car into the high street.

"No," he said. "I've brought all that with us. I forgot a few essentials, that's all. We could do with a stock of firelighters and matches for a start."

"*Firelighters?* But surely it's too hot even to think about lighting a fire!"

Dr Wainwright looked suddenly confused.

"It's a strange thing," he said, "but up at the manor it was really rather cold and miserable." He reversed into a parking space beside a small convenience store and turned off the engine. "In fact it was raining."

He opened the car door and got out. "I'll only be a few minutes. Are you OK waiting here?"

Rose nodded.

She watched her uncle disappear inside the shop and sat back in her seat.

It couldn't be as bad as all that at the manor, surely? Not with weather like this only a couple of miles down the road. Still, if the house hadn't been lived in for ages, it probably would feel a bit on the damp side, and a good fire would dry it out in no time. As for the rain, well, that wasn't going to last for long. It was probably just a passing shower.

She glanced down the high street to where a family had gathered under a blue-and-white-striped awning, each of them clutching an ice cream.

Now that was more like it. Perhaps she could persuade her uncle to buy her one of those before they set off. It would be the perfect thing to cool her down.

She leaned out of the car window, watching enviously.

Then she frowned. A familiar-looking figure had just come into view. It was the old man from the train, ambling towards her and sucking on a pipe.

Rose ducked back inside the car. The last thing she needed right now was more dire warnings about Gravenhunger Manor.

She kept her head down as he walked past, then sneaked a look behind her.

The old man paused for a moment outside a pub on the corner of the high street and took a final draw on his pipe. And then he tapped it out on a nearby bench and went inside.

Phoenix gazed out of the window at the curious-shaped mound on the other side of the river.

It felt so strange, standing here in the exact same place his mother had once stood, looking out at the same view – as if he had somehow been transported back in time. He half expected to turn round and find her there behind him.

He started, his eye caught by a flutter of movement just above his head. Glancing up, he saw a huge yellow moth trapped inside the top folds of the curtains.

Phoenix shuddered. Gravenhunger Manor might have been grand in its day, but it certainly wasn't any more. As far as he could make out, the whole house was falling apart.

He stepped away from the window and made for the stairs.

Fresh air. That was what he needed. Fresh air and then a proper night's sleep.

Letting himself out on to the landing, he shut the door behind him and headed down to the ground floor – past the grandfather clock, past the luggage in the hallway and out through the front door.

Of course, he really ought to be getting on with unpacking his stuff. But it wouldn't hurt to leave it a while longer, would it? At least he knew which room he was having.

Phoenix stood for a moment in the driveway, breathing in the rainy air, then set off round the back of the house towards the overgrown garden, which stretched for a hundred metres or so before merging with the forest beyond.

Not far from its border with the trees, a pair of swings was swaying from the branches of an old apple tree.

He made his way along the path towards them, past broken trellises and weed-infested vegetable beds, straggling brambles and drifts of tall nettles.

Reaching out, he ran his fingers over one of the wooden seats, recoiling as the edge of the swing crumbled away at his touch.

Who had last swung on these? His mother, perhaps? Had they been put up for her?

In the distance he could hear the hum of a car engine approaching down the track.

They were back – and any minute now Dad would be calling to him to come and say hello to Rose.

Well, his cousin would just have to wait. He didn't want to see anyone right now – least of all some sympathetic girl he hardly knew.

Phoenix darted out of the rain into the forest.

He was running now, dodging between the pines,

chasing through clearings, sliding down steep banks strewn with fallen pine cones and then up the other side, his breath coming in noisy rasps.

When at last he paused, bent nearly double and clutching his aching sides, he sensed daylight between the trees ahead. What was more, the noise of the car engine had disappeared ... and a new sound was pounding in his ears.

Guessing at what must lie ahead, he straightened up and hurried out into the rain.

Before him raged the river he had glimpsed from the attic window, and across it, not far from where he was standing, lay an ancient-looking fallen pine, its massive trunk straddling the wild grey water beneath.

Phoenix picked his way through the undergrowth towards it.

His father had asked him not to go beyond the garden, hadn't he?

But there was no way he was going back yet. Not until he could sneak in without being noticed and hide himself away in the little attic bedroom. Anyway, now he was here he might as well take a quick look. Get across the river and up the embankment on the other side. Check out that weird-shaped mound he had seen from the house.

He hitched himself on to the tree-trunk bridge and dug his knees into its sides.

He'd keep this little expedition to himself.

After all, secrets were what his family seemed to do best.

Rose peered inside the last of the fourth-floor bedrooms and sighed.

What on earth had possessed her uncle to take on a place like this over the summer? It had to be about the most depressing house she had ever set foot in.

From the outside it was grand enough — all fancy stonework and tall chimneys, but inside the rooms were dark and dusty, with long strips of wallpaper hanging off the walls. Patches of damp rose from the floors and the furniture had been draped in heavy sheets. It was just like something out of that spooky Victorian novel they'd started reading in class last term. Uncle Joel was kidding himself if he reckoned all it needed was a good airing.

He'd been right about the weather, though. After the blistering heat of the village, it didn't make sense at all. A cold wind whistled around the eaves and rain fell from a leaden sky.

She closed the door to the bedroom and clattered back down the stairs.

She'd been round the whole house twice now, trekking through the maze of corridors until her legs ached, and her cousin was nowhere to be seen. It wasn't like she'd been expecting a welcome party or anything, but at least he could have shown his face when she'd arrived. Surely that wouldn't have been too much to ask.

In the drawing room she could hear her uncle cursing over the fire he was trying to light in the huge stone hearth.

Poor Uncle Joel. He'd taken one look at the multiplying rain clouds when they had returned from the station and hurried off to light a fire, telling Rose to go and find Phoenix.

Well, she hadn't found him.

And there was no point spending any more time looking for him, either. He would turn up when he was good and ready. In the meantime, she might just as well get on with picking herself a bedroom: after all, there were enough to choose from.

First, though, she would make herself useful and wheel the bikes in out of the rain. She'd noticed a garden shed round the back of the house – they would be fine in there.

Emerging from the shed a few minutes later, Rose glanced up at the looming black clouds, then stopped still, her eye caught by a room tucked away in the eaves.

So there were *five* storeys to Gravenhunger Manor, not four...

She must have missed something. A door, maybe, with a staircase leading to another bedroom...

...the perfect place for her cousin to hide out.

Rose grinned to herself.

She shut the shed door and headed back towards the house.

There was no way Phoenix was going to escape that easily.

Phoenix slid off the tree-trunk bridge and fought his way through the rain-soaked undergrowth on the other side of the river. Already he was waist-high in nettles and brambles, which grasped at his bare arms, covering him in stings and scratches.

If only he had thought to bring a sweatshirt with him. At least that would have kept off some of the rain – and it was definitely cold enough to need one.

Ahead of him lay an embankment of earth, rising several metres from the riverbank.

He dug his fingers into the crumbling soil and pulled himself up it, then stared out across the broad sweep of land at the mound in front of him.

Close up, it looked more extraordinary than ever, jutting up out of the earth like some vast upturned wheelbarrow and covered all over in spiky tufts of grass.

Had his mother explored it, he wondered? She would have seen it from the attic window, surely – it was impossible to miss.

Phoenix started towards the mound, rain lashing his cheeks. As he approached it, a chill wind seemed to blow up out of nowhere, whipping the grass around him into a wild frenzy and marooning him on a sea of billowing green.

He scrambled up the side, slipping and sliding on the wet grass.

At the top he stiffened. Someone was watching him, he was sure of it.

He spun round, his heart racing.

But there was only the sea over to the south, barely visible through the rain and the fast-descending mist, and behind him the dark chimneys of Gravenhunger Manor.

He gave himself a shake. Really, he shouldn't be so taken in by the place. Just because he was in the middle of nowhere and the weather was closing in on him didn't mean he needed to get all spooked out, did it?

And then he frowned.

Not far from where he was standing, something seemed to be moving above the surface of the mound – an odd thickening in the mist that appeared, just for a moment, to be almost human in shape.

He rubbed his eyes and looked again … but it had gone.

Phoenix cursed to himself.

This was ridiculous. He was tired, that was all. Tired and wrung out. And who could blame him, after everything he'd been through in the past twenty-four hours. It was time to get back to the house before Dad wondered where he'd got to. Shift his things into the attic bedroom and clean himself up a bit. Maybe even crash out for a few hours before dinner.

He should never have allowed himself to get distracted. He wasn't here to traipse around the grounds getting soaked to the skin, was he? He was here to find out what had happened to his mother all those years ago. And that meant heading back and starting to look for some clues.

Phoenix turned to leave the mound.

He had just reached the edge when his foot caught inside a burrow and he went slamming to the ground.

Staggering upright, his gaze flickered back to the grey walls of the manor, and he caught his breath.

Someone was moving at the attic window.

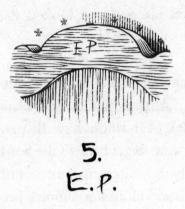

5.
E.P.

Phoenix burst in through the front door and made straight for the stairs.

"Hey!" exclaimed Dr Wainwright, poking his head out of the drawing room, a box of matches in his hand. "Where are you going in such a hurry? Did Rose find you? I sent her to look for you."

Phoenix didn't reply.

He charged up the stairs, taking them two at a time and not pausing for breath until he reached the tapestry at the top of the fourth-floor staircase.

The door to the secret stairwell was shut, but he could tell she was up there. Muffled banging and scraping noises echoed from the floorboards above his head, and there was music too. The steady beat of some rubbish girl band pulsing away on a tinny portable stereo system.

He grabbed hold of the brass doorknob, his blood boiling.

She had no business being in there. She had no *right*.

True, he hadn't left any sign that he'd been up there already and bagged the attic for himself. But that room had belonged to his mother – and that meant it was now his. It was perfectly simple.

Not that he was about to tell Rose that. Until he knew exactly what had happened here all those years ago, he wasn't going to tell anybody anything.

Phoenix thundered up the stairs.

"What d'you think you're doing?" he yelled, thrusting open the door. "This is my room, OK? You'll have to find somewhere else to sleep!"

His cousin turned towards him and her face zoomed into focus – a face framed by a cascade of red curls and illuminated by the most astonishing pair of blue eyes.

For a moment neither of them moved, Rose open-mouthed beside the chest of drawers, Phoenix frozen on the threshold.

Then Rose reached down and flicked off the switch to her stereo.

"Well, hello to you too," she said into the silence that followed. "It's generally a good idea to knock first, you know." She leaned back against the chest of drawers and crossed her arms. "It's kind of more polite that way."

The air bristled between them.

"I … I…" stammered Phoenix.

His eyes flitted over the newly made-up bed … the rucksack lying on the bare floorboards … the clothes spewing from its loosened top … the pile of books beside the bed … the kicked-off trainers in one corner of the room.

This wasn't turning out as he'd expected.

He'd thought it would just be a matter of telling his cousin what was what. Of waiting while she gathered up her things and then booting her out of the attic as quickly as he could. But now he was actually here, standing face to face with her, things felt rather different. Rose didn't look like she was about to be booted out of anywhere by anyone. Least of all by him.

Right now she was looking around the room and frowning to herself.

"Anyway, what d'you mean it's yours?" she said. "I can't see any of your stuff in here. Your bag's still down in the hallway with your dad's."

Phoenix dropped his gaze.

"Look," he muttered, "I found this room first, all right? I discovered the entrance to the stairwell when

Dad was out collecting you from the station."

Rose let out a short laugh.

"So?" she said. "That counts for nothing. Just because you found it first, doesn't mean it belongs to you, does it? I found it too, remember. And like I said, it was totally empty when I got here."

Phoenix continued to glare down at the floor, his eyes now glued to a long run of woodworm etched into one of the bare boards.

"I meant to move my things up right away," he said. "Honestly. It's just…"

He broke off, stabbing at the woodworm with the toe of his trainer.

"I needed some fresh air after the long journey. I thought I'd go out and explore the grounds."

"You mean you decided to go over to that mound on the other side of the river," corrected Rose. "I did see you there, you know."

Phoenix shrugged. "Whatever. It doesn't really matter where I went, does it? The point is I didn't mean to leave it so long before coming back up here and unpacking my stuff."

"You don't give up, do you? What is it about this room, hey? What makes it so special?"

"There's nothing special about it. I just fancy being this high up, that's all. I like the view."

"Yeah, right," said Rose. She gestured through the

open door towards the stairwell and the labyrinth of rooms that lay beyond. "What's wrong with one of the other rooms?" she asked. "There's one on the first floor with a four-poster bed. It's much bigger than this one. I was going to choose it myself, but I thought your dad might like it. Why don't you ask him if you can have it?"

Phoenix glanced up.

"I'll tell you what," he said, meeting his cousin's gaze at last. "How about I ask him if *you* can have it? He won't care where he sleeps, and that way we'll both get what we want, won't we?"

Rose regarded her cousin coolly. "Maybe I don't want that room now. Maybe I want to stay exactly where I am."

Phoenix dug his fingernails into the palms of his hands. "You'd be doing me a favour…"

Rose shook her head. "Sorry, Phoenix. You haven't exactly put me in the mood for favours." She kicked aside her rucksack and advanced towards him. "I'm not budging. I'm halfway through unpacking now. And anyway, I like this room. It's kind of secret."

Phoenix backed away, half falling down the top step of the narrow staircase as his cousin grasped hold of the door handle.

"But—"

"I *said* I'm not moving."

The door closed, and Phoenix stood there for a moment in the darkness, his pulse racing.

Then he set off down the stairs, thrusting his hand into his pocket for the comfort of the little silver angel.

But it was empty.

Rose threw herself down on the bed, sneezing as a cloud of dust loosened itself from the faded patchwork quilt and settled all around her.

Who on earth did her cousin think he was, barging in on her like that?

This room didn't *belong* to anyone.

Like she'd told him, there'd been nothing in it when she'd found it, and in any case, it wasn't as if it was the only bedroom in the place. There had to be about twenty others, most of them way bigger than this one.

Not that she was especially bothered about having it for herself. In fact if her cousin had knocked on the door and asked for the room nicely, she probably would have given it to him straight off.

But he hadn't asked for it nicely. He hadn't even come close.

No – she might feel sorry for him, but there was no excuse for behaving like that.

She rolled over on to her side and switched on her mobile. Perhaps she'd text Mum and Dad and fill them in on things so far.

Great. There was no reception. Not even a single bar. She'd just have to try in a different part of the house later on. She'd go mad if she couldn't even keep in touch with people this summer.

Rose reached out with one hand to where two tiny letters had been carved into the headboard.

She traced them with the tip of her finger.

E.P.

The initials of some visitor to the house, maybe. A child, most probably, with nothing better to do than scratch their name into the wood.

Outside, the rain hammered against the loose glass of the windowpane and the wind whistled around the eaves.

Rose sighed.

What with a pig-headed cousin, an old wreck of a house and a generous helping of rubbish weather thrown in for good measure, she reckoned she had the perfect ingredients for the worst holiday on record.

Well, she'd give it a week. One week.

And then she was out of here.

"You're very quiet, Phoenix."

Phoenix looked up from his soup bowl and met his father's gaze.

"And you haven't touched your supper. Are you feeling all right?"

"I'm fine," mumbled Phoenix. "Just not very hungry, that's all."

He trailed his spoon over the soup. Apart from the sandwiches they had grabbed at a service station on the way down, he hadn't eaten a thing all day, but the thought of swallowing a single mouthful right now made his stomach churn.

How could he when he'd gone and lost the one thing that really mattered to him – his mother's precious keepsake?

It could be anywhere.

Or at least anywhere between the attic bedroom and the mound.

It might have fallen out of his pocket on his way across the driveway or the garden or the forest … or even on his slippery journey over the tree-trunk bridge, in which case it would be lost for ever in the dark depths of the river.

"It's not exactly a feast, I know," sighed Dr Wainwright, still watching his son. "I'd planned on making us something special, but I'm afraid the oven's broken along with everything else in this damned place. I can't even get the fire to light properly. The drawing room's just one great big smoky mess. I've had to leave the windows open to let out the smell."

He shivered and turned to his niece.

"I'm sorry, Rose. I didn't think it was going to be anything like this bad down here. But things are OK with you otherwise, are they? You've chosen yourself a room and everything?"

Rose nodded. "I'm all sorted, thanks, Uncle Joel. I'm really pleased with the one I've picked."

She smiled sweetly at Phoenix, who scowled back at her.

Dr Wainwright frowned.

He glanced from Rose to Phoenix and then at Rose again.

"Am I missing something here?" he asked. "You two have actually said hello to one another, haven't you?"

Phoenix pushed aside his bowl.

"Oh yes," he said. "Don't you worry about that, Dad. We've said hello all right."

"Good," said Dr Wainwright. "I wouldn't like to think there was any – er – awkwardness between the pair of you."

He finished his soup and stood up from the table.

"I'm off to get on with a bit of work. Could you two clear up, d'you think? And then I reckon we could all do with an early night. I'm sure we'll feel a whole lot better in the morning."

He polished his glasses on the sleeve of his sweater.

"Talking of tomorrow, I'm going to have to go back into the village first thing. I need to find someone to come and unblock the chimney. The boiler looks like it hasn't worked in ages, and we'll have to keep the place warm somehow, especially if this weather doesn't improve."

They all turned towards the kitchen window, where fingers of rain were streaking their way down the glass, only to be blown off course by the howling gale.

"I just don't understand it," said Dr Wainwright, replacing his glasses. "It was so lovely in the village. In fact there was nothing but bright sunshine all the way back from the station. Right up until the turning for the manor."

He crossed to the far end of the kitchen and began pulling down the tattered old blinds.

"Anyway, that's what I'm up to tomorrow, if either of you wants to tag along. I'm sure you'd find something to keep you occupied in the village. There's a promenade and an arcade – and a museum too, I think…"

"No thanks," cut in Phoenix. "I'll stay here, if that's OK. There's – there's things I need to do."

His father turned to face him. "Like what exactly?"

Phoenix flushed. "I just want to hang out, that's all. Get to know the place a bit."

Rose eyed her cousin across the table.

"In that case I'll stay too," she said. "I wouldn't want to, you know, *miss out* on anything."

Dr Wainwright looked at them both. "Fair enough. You do whatever you want. But don't forget what I said to you earlier, Phoenix. No serious exploring without me, OK? Same applies to you, Rose. I don't want you going any further afield than the garden."

Rose needled Phoenix with a steely blue gaze.

"Of course not," she said, her eyes burning into her cousin. "Wouldn't dream of it. Besides, I'm sure we can find plenty of things to do inside the house."

Phoenix gritted his teeth.

His cousin had to be the most annoying person on the planet.

Still, she hadn't grassed on him about where he'd been this afternoon, had she? He'd give her that at least.

He scraped his chair back from the table and began to gather up the bowls and plates.

How could he have been so careless as to lose the silver angel? And just when he should have been concentrating on solving his mother's mystery too. He could have spent tomorrow getting on with a really thorough search of the house, for a start. And it wouldn't have hurt to take a trip down to the village either. There was no knowing what he might find out about the past if he asked around a bit.

Now, though, all that would have to wait.

Until the angel was back in his pocket he couldn't afford to think about anything else.

In the morning, just as soon as Dad had left for the village, he would retrace every one of his steps until he had found it. And if that meant disobeying his father for a second time ... well, that was exactly what he was going to do.

6.
IN MEMORIAM

Rose stood at the attic window and looked out through the grey morning mist.

She wrapped her arms around herself and shivered.

It didn't matter how many extra layers she put on, she couldn't seem to get warm. Everything about Gravenhunger Manor felt damp and cold: the floors, the walls, even the air inside it. And it was the same outside: nothing but mist and drizzle. Over towards the horizon, though, it was different. Beyond the river and the strange-shaped mound she could see sunlight – wonderful, glittering sunlight – spilt like a pool of liquid gold over the distant sea.

She'd been watching her cousin since just after breakfast, and whatever it was he was doing over there, he was certainly taking his time about it.

He'd come sloping round the back of the house the moment Uncle Joel had left for the village. He'd crossed the garden towards the forest, pausing briefly beside the wooden swings and glancing up towards the attic, as if he knew perfectly well that he was being tracked.

Rose had whipped back behind the moth-eaten curtains, but probably not before he had spotted her.

Still, what did it matter?

He had seen her staring at him on the mound yesterday, hadn't he? It wasn't going to come as any great surprise that she was watching him again today.

It was hard to be completely certain, what with the rain and the mist and the general murkiness, but it looked very much as if Phoenix was searching for something.

He'd been pacing up and down the mound for nearly an hour now, stopping every so often to focus on one particular area near the edge, his hands spread over his knees, his head bent towards the ground.

Rose sighed.

What was it about this odd-shaped hump of earth that everyone seemed so interested in?

First there'd been the old man on the train, telling her to keep away from it, and now here was Phoenix poring all over it.

Clearly the business about the place being haunted

was just a load of nonsense. But what if there was something at least interesting about Gravenhunger Manor and its grounds? And what if Phoenix knew all about it?

Well, one thing was for sure – he wasn't going to share any valuable nuggets of information with her. Since their head-to-head in the attic yesterday, they hadn't uttered a single word to each other.

Rose turned away from the window.

There was nothing more infuriating than being left out of a secret.

She flopped down on the end of her bed, then jerked back upright.

Of course! The guidebook! Surely the mound would be mentioned in that.

Dragging her rucksack out from underneath the bed, she slid back the zip on the top pocket and drew out the booklet.

Perhaps – just perhaps – she was about to get some answers.

Phoenix checked his watch.

Eleven-thirty already.

A whole hour of trudging up and down in the pouring rain, and so far he had found nothing.

His plan the previous evening had been to retrace

his steps from the house to the mound, starting on the fourth-floor landing just outside the hidden entrance to the attic room. But then it had dawned on him in the middle of the night that the most likely place the little angel would be was where he had tripped and caught his foot in the burrow at the edge of the mound. It made sense to look there first.

He pulled the hood of his waterproof down over his forehead and stared at the ground once more.

He had scoured the area around the burrow again and again, parting the tufts of grass and combing the sandy soil with the tips of his fingers, but there was no sign of the angel. He was going to have to go back to the house soon and dry off before Dad returned from the village. He could always sneak out again later on. A lot later on, if necessary – once it had grown dark and everyone had gone to bed. At least then his nosy-parker cousin wouldn't be watching him out of the window, as she was almost certainly doing right now.

Phoenix made to leave the mound, then froze.

A shape was drifting towards him, a shape which seemed at first glance to be no more than a rogue patch of mist, blown this way and that by the buffeting wind, but as he stared harder seemed to take on the form of a human silhouette.

So he hadn't been seeing things yesterday…

For a moment he just stood there, his brain

screaming at him to run – but his legs felt like jelly.

Now the shape was coming closer … and suddenly he was scrambling down the side of the mound, not knowing what it was that he was running from, knowing only that he had to get away…

Halfway to the embankment he glanced back.

The silhouette was still there, flitting over the surface, its outline pale and blurred … but very definitely human.

Phoenix raced on towards the river.

At the crest of the embankment he paused, bent double from a stitch in his side and gasping for breath.

He blinked.

Directly below him something bright was scudding down the river … something silvery-white…

Dropping to his knees, he craned forward, but already he could see that the brightness was nothing but the foaming water itself, taunting and teasing him with the illusion of a thousand silvery angels.

How could he have been so stupid? If the angel had dropped out while he was crossing the tree-trunk bridge, he was hardly going to find it floating on the surface of the river, was he? It would be lying at the bottom, unreachable amongst the weeds and the mud and the rocks.

He twisted round and lowered himself over the

edge of the embankment, his view of the mound slowly slipping from view.

On its flattened top the strange silhouette had become eerily still...

...as if it was watching his every movement.

Rose ran up the narrow staircase to the attic.

Lunchtime had been a total nightmare.

Apart from one remark Uncle Joel had made about the brilliant sunshine down in the village that morning, no one had said a thing.

They had sat round the kitchen table in silence, and if it hadn't been for the chimney sweep arriving, Rose reckoned they would have stayed there all afternoon, their moods darkening by the minute.

It wasn't what she was used to, that was for sure. You could barely get a word in edgeways at home, what with Mum and Dad rabbiting on about this, that and the other. Here at Gravenhunger Manor it was a miracle if her cousin and uncle managed to exchange more than a few words.

Still, she'd managed to escape at last.

Uncle Joel was getting on with some more work and the chimney sweep had disappeared into the drawing room with a collection of peculiar-looking brushes, muttering to himself about the weather.

Where Phoenix had gone, she wasn't sure.

For a moment she wondered whether he might have dared to go straight back over to the mound. But there was no sign of him out of the window. And in any case, the rain was getting worse by the minute. No one in their right mind would be out there in that.

Rose sprawled on top of her bed and opened the guidebook. She'd only managed a quick look through before lunch, and so far she'd found no information about the mound at all.

She flicked past the list of tourist attractions ... past the map of the seafront ... past the names and addresses of places to stay...

And then she paused.

Near the back, tucked away in the corner of the page, was something she'd missed: a small photo of the mound – and beneath it, a couple of lines of text.

She pressed the pages flat and started to read.

Believed to be an old burial site, the mound in the grounds of Gravenhunger Manor dates from Anglo-Saxon times. Rumour has it that the place is haunted and local people regard the area with some disquiet.

She snapped the book shut.

So much for thinking there might be something interesting about the mound. It was just an ancient hump of earth, that was all. The inhabitants of Gravenhunger obviously led such boring lives they had to invent stupid ghost stories to keep themselves amused … and the old man she'd met on the train was no exception.

As for Phoenix, well, she was no closer to understanding her cousin's odd behaviour than she had been before she'd opened the guidebook. Even if he'd read something similar and got it into his head that the mound was haunted, it didn't explain what he'd been doing walking up and down all over it.

Rose sighed.

This whole holiday had been a terrible mistake. The weather was atrocious, her uncle was working all the time and she and Phoenix weren't even on speaking terms. At least if they'd been talking they could have been listening to music or playing a board game together. True, she could think of better ways of spending what was supposed to be a glorious summer. But it would be a definite improvement on sitting around all by herself.

Perhaps it was time to put yesterday behind them.

Perhaps it was time to call a bit of a truce.

Snatches of conversation were drifting up through the floorboards into his bedroom, and Phoenix didn't like the sound of what he was hearing.

"I don't know what to make of it," the chimney sweep was saying. "I've been sweeping that chimney for nearly three hours now and I can't get the blasted thing working for love nor money."

"I thought it was just me," Phoenix heard his father reply. "I spent ages trying to light a fire yesterday and all I got was a huge cloud of smoke and a great big mess. I really am getting pretty fed up with this place, and the awful weather isn't helping. I'm about ready to ditch the whole thing and head home."

Phoenix sat down on the four-poster bed, his heart clenching.

Leave? Already? Without the silver angel? And before he'd had a chance to find out what had happened here?

"It's certainly got a climate of its own," agreed the sweep. "I'm not one for village gossip myself, but they do say it does nothing but rain up here."

There was a clattering of poles and brushes, then the sound of footsteps as the two men left the drawing room and went out into the hallway.

A minute later there was a knock at the bedroom door.

"Who is it?" called Phoenix, jumping to his feet.

He scowled as his cousin's head appeared round the side of the door.

"Oh," he said. "It's you. What d'you want?"

Rose blushed. "I was wondering whether you wanted to do something together. You know, to help pass the time."

"Like what exactly?" said Phoenix suspiciously.

"I don't know. It's too wet to go out on the bikes. But we could play a board game if you like. Let's face it, there's not much else to do around here, is there?"

"Are you saying you don't like this house? Are you saying there's something wrong with it?"

"*Something wrong with it?* Oh, come off it! This has got to be about the coldest, dampest, most miserable place I've ever been to in my life. If we left tomorrow it wouldn't be a moment too soon."

Phoenix bristled. "You should count yourself lucky you were invited down here at all. You wouldn't have gone anywhere this summer otherwise, would you?"

Rose shrugged. "Probably not. But anything would have been better than this."

"Well, it's not my problem you're bored," said Phoenix, crossing the room towards her. "It wasn't *my* idea for you to come. I would have much preferred it if it had just been me and Dad."

And before his cousin could open her mouth to reply, he had shut the door firmly in her face.

77

Rose stood on the landing, her heart thumping against her chest.

So much for a truce. Phoenix had to be about the touchiest person she'd ever met.

Rummaging in her jeans pocket, she pulled out her phone. If only she could contact her parents, then perhaps they might agree to let her come home. Especially if they knew things were as bad as this.

But it was the same here as in every other room she'd tried – the little bars at the top of the screen steadfastly refused to spring to life.

She trailed downstairs.

In the hallway everything was quiet. The door to the drawing room was open, but there was no one about. The chimney sweep must have gone home, and her uncle was probably still working.

Rose opened the front door and stood under the old hurricane lamp, listening to the rain pounding on the driveway and scowling down at her mobile.

Still nothing.

At this rate she'd have to cadge a lift with Uncle Joel next time he went into the village and find a phone box. There had to be *some* way of getting through to Mum and Dad.

She turned to go back inside, then stopped.

In amongst the hammering of the rain and the screeching of the wind, she could hear a creaking noise coming from the forest to the left of the manor.

Pulling up the hood of her fleece, she set off round the side of the house and plunged into the thickly clustered pines, grateful for their canopy of evergreen.

The noise was getting louder and clearer now … and not far off something was visible between the trees.

Another few steps and she was standing right in front of it – a small grey building emblazoned with a cross … a chapel hidden amongst the pines, its door creaking back and forth in the wind.

Rose picked her way towards it, eyeing the clusters of moss-encrusted gravestones around her. When she reached the chapel door, she pulled the iron latch towards her and stepped inside.

She stood quite still in the darkness, breathing in the musty scent and staring up at the single stained-glass window, a circular mosaic of greens and reds and blues and golds.

Slowly, her eyes adjusted to the gloom.

The tiny chapel was lined with wooden pews, each one boxed in with a little door of its own. At the top of the nave stood a plain stone font, and beyond the pulpit lay a pair of alabaster tombs – some long-dead lord and lady of the manor probably, their hands clasped in death.

Rose jumped as a violent gust of wind slammed the door behind her.

She steadied herself against a nearby pew, then raised her eyes to where, just a short distance up the nave, a small, modern-looking bronze plaque glinted on the whitewashed wall.

Tiptoeing across the floor, she craned forward and scanned the stark black lettering.

IN MEMORY OF OUR ANGEL
LOST BUT NOT FORGOTTEN

Rose turned and hurried back down the nave.

She pushed her way out into the open and huddled into her fleece.

But it wasn't the cold that was making her shiver.

7.
UNDER THE
FLOORBOARD

Phoenix peered through the gap in the banisters.

If only Dad would hurry up and go to bed.

This had to be about the sixth time he had crept up to the second-floor landing, and still the line of light under his father's bedroom door was as bright as ever.

He skulked back down the stairs and returned to his room.

The silver angel had to be out there somewhere, it just *had* to be. He hadn't looked in the right place yet, that was all. He needed to revert to his original plan and retrace his steps one by one. Work his way round to the back of the house, past the swings at the bottom of the garden and out into the forest.

But he had to do it soon … he had to find the angel tonight. Dad was losing patience with

Gravenhunger Manor, that much was obvious, and the rate things were going they might not be here much longer.

He slumped down on the edge of the four-poster bed and buried his head in his hands.

What a mess he'd made of everything. He was supposed to be getting to the bottom of his mother's terrible secret, and so far all he'd managed to do was lose his last connection with her. Things couldn't have turned out any worse if he'd tried.

And then there was Rose. He hadn't exactly got off to a flying start with her either. What had got into him earlier, biting her head off like that, when all she'd done was ask him if he wanted to hang out with her? It was hardly reasonable behaviour.

Well, tomorrow would be different. Tomorrow he would try and be pleasant to Rose – and what was more, if he'd found the angel by then, he would get his act together and discover what had happened here. Whatever it took, he would unlock the door to his mother's mysterious past.

Phoenix stood up from the bed.

Maybe he should just take a chance. Sneak off outside while his father was still awake. After all, it wasn't very likely he was going to come down and check on him, was it? He'd never exactly been the saying-goodnight sort.

But then again, what if he *did* come down? What if he chose tonight to break the habit of a lifetime and knocked on the door only to find the room empty? There'd be hell to pay then. And there'd be questions too. Lots of them. Questions which he didn't feel in the least like answering.

Footsteps sounded on the landing above and Phoenix dived into bed, pulling the covers up over his head.

He could hear the bathroom door opening ... a tap being turned on and off ... then the door re-opening and footsteps padding back across the landing.

Perhaps this time he was in luck.

He lay there for a while in the darkness, his eyes wide open, then relaxed as a rhythmic snore began to resonate through the floorboards.

At last! It sounded like Dad was well away, and luckily he had always been a heavy sleeper.

Phoenix scrambled out of bed and switched on the bedside lamp. He pulled his clothes on over his pyjamas and put on his waterproof.

Then he rolled up a spare blanket and pushed it down under the covers, prodding it into position until it was roughly human in shape.

Just in case, he thought, picking up his torch and flicking off the lamp. *Just in case.*

Every time Rose closed her eyes she was back in the little chapel in the forest, staring at the words on the bronze plaque until they were burned like scars into her brain: *In memory of our angel, lost but not forgotten.*

She pressed her face into the pillow and shuddered.

It was the angel bit that did it. A word like that had to refer to a child, surely? But why not call the child by its name? And why were there no dates on the inscription? It was so bare. So empty-looking.

Outside the wind raged and the rain rattled like gunfire against the glass. It seemed the storm was working itself up into a frenzy.

Rose sat up. She might just as well get out of bed and have a look. Anything to take her mind off those creepy words.

She padded over to the window and pulled back the curtains, then blinked.

Zigzagging across the garden was the beam of a torch…

Squinting down, she watched the narrow shaft of light sweep in silent strokes over the drenched grass.

What was Phoenix playing at? What on earth could be so important that he needed to go out there in the dead of night?

The torchbeam circled the pair of swings at the far end of the garden before moving off once more. There was the occasional morse-like flash as her cousin picked his way through the trees on the outskirts of the forest … and then he was swallowed up into the beckoning arms of the pines, and all she could see was darkness.

Whatever he did, he mustn't give up.

True, he'd nearly reached the end of the forest and hadn't found the silver angel yet. But there was still the last bit of woodland left to check … and then the undergrowth on either side of the river and the stretch of land beyond.

Phoenix paused for a moment, rubbing his eyes.

It wouldn't be such a bad idea to look over the mound again either. Shine his torch right inside that burrow. There was always the chance he had missed something earlier.

He stared out through the trees, his skin creeping as he remembered the strange silhouette he had glimpsed that morning.

Was it possible he had seen a ghost of some kind? He'd never believed in such things before, but the outline of the shape had definitely been human, and there was no point pretending otherwise.

If it *was* a ghost, then what was it doing on the mound? Could it really and truly have sensed his presence? And what if it was still there ... waiting for him?

He hesitated.

It would be so easy to turn back now. In less than five minutes he could be inside the house and safe under the covers again. But that was hardly going to find his mother's angel, was it?

Pointing his torch back towards the forest floor, he trudged on in the direction of the roaring river.

He needed to get a grip on himself – and fast.

It was the memory of his mother that mattered. Not some stupid *thing* that probably didn't even exist.

Rose reached behind her and dragged the quilt off the bed.

The house was growing colder by the minute and outside the rain seemed to have turned to sleet. What was wrong with this place? It was supposed to be summer.

Wrapping the quilt round her shoulders, she knelt down beside the window and checked her cousin's progress.

It had seemed like an age before he had finally emerged from the forest. She had even begun to wonder whether he had got lost amongst the army of pines, and when at last a tiny light had appeared on the other side of the river, a surge of something that felt very much like relief had coursed through her.

She watched as the beam of light advanced up the side of the mound, cutting through the sleet in the same sweeping, scouring motion.

It stilled at the place Phoenix had lingered beside that morning, then disappeared completely, as if it was being focused right down inside the earth.

Shifting slightly, she knelt up to get a better look, then jerked back.

The floorboard she was kneeling on felt warm…

Rose moved to one side and ran her hand over its woodwormy surface. The board was loose at one end.

She bent down beside it, her pulse quickening … and sliding the tips of her fingers under its free edge, levered it towards her.

Phoenix shone his torch into the burrow.

There was definitely something down there.

Whether or not it was the silver angel he couldn't be sure – it was a long way down and almost totally covered in sandy soil. But it certainly looked about the right size and glinted in the torchlight if he got the angle just so.

He pressed himself flat against the wet ground and reached into the hole with his free hand. The air inside was warm, and what was more, the further in he stretched the warmer it seemed to become. It was as if the object was giving out a heat all of its own.

There was no way he could get to it, though. It had to be a couple of metres down at least. He would have to clear away some of the soil at the surface before he stood a chance of even touching it. And it wasn't going to be easy, either. This section of the mound was riddled with animal holes – one false move and the earth would come toppling in on itself.

Heaving himself back on to his knees, Phoenix focused the torch on the edge of the burrow and began to scoop away the soil with his bare hands…

…and behind him, hidden in the veil of falling sleet, hovered the pale silhouette.

Rose snatched her hand away and the floorboard flipped back into place.

She shook the film of grime and dust from her fingers, her skin prickling all over.

Whatever it was that was down there had felt hard and warm and – dare she even think it? – *alive*.

Steadying herself against the wall, she glanced out of the window once more.

The torchbeam had reappeared on the mound and the light was being focused in the same place as before.

Rose scrambled to her feet.

Light! Of course! That was what she needed! Light would make everything OK again. Light would make everything normal. She stumbled across the room and flicked on the light switch.

Nothing.

What? The electricity had been working fine earlier on. There must have been a power cut. Well, that was typical, wasn't it?

She fumbled inside her rucksack for her torch and crossed back to the window.

It was no good – she was going to have to find out what was underneath that loose floorboard. She couldn't just sit around all night wondering.

Gingerly she lifted it up and shone the torch inside the cavity between the attic floor and the ceiling below.

And then she caught her breath.

In amongst the dirt and the cobwebs was a rusty old iron bolt…

…and it was glowing.

8.
THE CONNECTION

How or why he suddenly sensed it he didn't know.

The silhouette made no sound as it shimmered behind him. But in the time it took Phoenix to turn from the edge of the burrow and register its presence, he had lost his balance and fallen back against the fragile surface of the mound.

His arms jerked upwards … the torch catapulted from his hand … and beneath the weight of his fall the tunnel-ridden earth began to crumble in upon itself.

Grab something! Anything! Get a hold of the edge!

But there was nothing to grab hold of … nothing to keep him from falling into the burrow.

He glimpsed the shadowy silhouette above him … a fragment of sleety sky … and then there was nothing but raining earth and darkness.

Another second and she would never have seen it happen.

She had turned to look out of the window, the strange iron bolt now lying beside her on the sill, and watched as her cousin's torchbeam shot up through the darkness, then plummeted to the ground and died.

Rose pressed her face against the glass, willing the light to reappear.

Something was wrong out there, she just knew it.

It was as if Phoenix had simply lost control of the torch … as if something had startled him.

She waited another few moments, then twisted round from the window and began tugging on her clothes, her fingers fumbling over the zips and buttons.

There was nothing else for it.

She was going to have to get over there herself.

Rose pulled on her waterproof and glanced around the attic bedroom.

She picked up her torch and reached for the iron bolt on the windowsill, brushing the cobwebs from its glowing surface and pushing it into her jeans pocket.

Exactly what it was, she had no idea.

But she wasn't going to let it out of her sight.

Phoenix jolted to a halt at the bottom of the burrow and opened his mouth in a silent scream.

He was going to be buried alive…

Earth was piling up on top of him faster than he could clear it away, squeezing the breath from his lungs.

He thrust out with his hands, clawing at the collapsing sides for something to grab hold of … but each time he was driven back by another torrent of cascading soil.

It was hot down here too … so hot he could scarcely breathe what little air there was, and beneath him one of his legs was growing numb with cramp.

He winced as something hard and sharp gouged into his thigh.

The silver angel…

Phoenix scrabbled blindly beneath him, seeking out the cool silver of his mother's keepsake.

But his fingers met instead with a strange and otherworldly warmth.

Rose thundered through the forest, her torch illuminating a trail of scuffed-up earth and pine needles between the trees.

Her cousin had certainly done a good job of showing her the way…

Not far off she could hear the rushing of water, and moments later she was bursting out into the freezing air and skidding to a standstill beside a huge fallen pine tree.

The river was wider than she'd imagined – much wider. And this tree trunk had to be how Phoenix had crossed it.

Vaulting on to the makeshift bridge, she began to shuffle across, the soles of her trainers skimming the seething surface below.

She jumped off on to the opposite bank and stumbled through the undergrowth towards the embankment, then jammed the torch between her teeth and heaved herself up it.

At the top she paused to catch her breath.

She was far enough away from the house to call to him now, surely? Her uncle would never hear her from this side of the river.

"Phoenix!" she yelled. "*Phoenix!*"

But though she strained her ears against the vast darkness, his answer never came.

It was only the faintest of sounds, but it was enough to ignite in Phoenix a tiny flicker of hope.

Somebody was out there! Somebody had called his name!

There it was again – small and muffled, but closer this time. Much closer.

He lunged against the weight of earth on top of him, the object he had mistaken for the silver angel clenched in his fist.

And then he felt it … a hand plunging through the earth towards him and grasping his own, wrenching him free and pulling him towards the surface.

"*Phoenix!*"

His cousin was kneeling over him, brushing the soil from his hair and his eyes.

"*What happened?*"

Phoenix opened his mouth to speak, but his body convulsed in a violent fit of choking. He writhed on the ground, retching up hard gobbets of earth.

"How did you know I was over here?" he spluttered at last. "How did you know I was in trouble?"

Rose sat back and wiped her hands on her jeans.

"I couldn't sleep," she said, picking up her torch from the edge of the burrow. "I got up and saw you going over to the mound. And then your torch flew up into the air, like you'd been scared or something. And, well, I just knew I had to get over here as fast as I could."

Phoenix struggled up on to his elbows and scanned the sleety darkness for the silhouette, but he could see nothing.

"What is it?" Rose asked. "What are you looking for?" She looked at him more closely. "I'm right, aren't I? Something did freak you out earlier. That's why you let go of the torch. What happened? Did someone follow you out here?"

"Of course not," mumbled Phoenix.

He forced his attention back to Rose.

"I'd been searching for something I'd dropped yesterday, OK? I reckoned it might have fallen down a burrow. But this part of the mound is full of animal holes, and when I tried to reach it the earth gave way beneath me. That's when I let go of the torch. It was as simple as that."

"What was it you'd lost?" asked Rose.

"Something my mother gave me. A – a little silver angel."

"An *angel*?"

Phoenix narrowed his eyes at his cousin. "Have you got a problem with that? Mum gave it to me just before she died, if you must know. It was special to me."

Rose gestured towards his clenched fist. "I take it you found it, then?"

"I thought I had," said Phoenix. "I thought I saw it glinting up at me from the bottom of the burrow. But it wasn't the angel. It was something else. Something a bit weird, actually."

He opened his fist and they both gazed down into the palm of his hand.

Lying there, half covered in earth, was a rusty iron bolt.

"It's warm," said Phoenix, holding it out to Rose. "Hot, even. Just like the earth I found it in. Here – feel it. What do you think it is?"

Rose didn't answer.

She was pulling something out of her jeans pocket and placing it beside the object in her cousin's hand...

...an identical glowing bolt.

"Where did you get that?" exclaimed Phoenix. "Have you been over here too?"

Rose shook her head. "I found it in the house about twenty minutes ago. Just before you fell into the burrow. It was underneath a loose floorboard in my bedroom."

"In your *bedroom*?" echoed Phoenix. "In *Mum's* bedroom?"

Rose blinked at him. "*What?*"

There was a moment's silence.

Phoenix placed the two bolts side by side on the mound and trailed his finger over them.

"Gravenhunger Manor used to belong to my mother," he said softly, his eyes fixed upon the bolts. "She lived here for a while when she was a child. That's why we're here."

Rose gaped.

"To your *mother*? But that's not what your dad said. He told me you were looking after the place for someone over the summer. A friend, I thought."

"That's because I asked him not to say anything," said Phoenix. "He only told me about it a couple of days ago, and I needed some time to get my head around it all. Even Dad didn't know about the house until the solicitor's stuff came through a few weeks after Mum died."

Rose stared past him into the thickening sleet, a glazed expression on her face.

"Of course," she murmured. "The initials in the headboard. So that's what they stand for…"

"Initials?"

"E.P.," explained Rose. "Your mother's initials. They're scratched into the bed in the attic." She looked back at her cousin. "I still don't understand, though. Why would your mother want to keep a house a secret?"

Phoenix picked up the bolt he had found at the bottom of the burrow and began to scratch away the surface covering of earth.

"Just before we came down here I found a letter," he said. "A letter my mum had written to Dad shortly before she died."

He paused.

"Perhaps I shouldn't be telling you this. It feels weird talking about it. Like I'm breaking Mum's trust or something."

"Oh, please go on. I won't say anything to anyone, I promise…"

Phoenix prised away the last of the earth and rubbed the bolt on the sleeve of his waterproof.

"In the letter it said that something terrible had happened here when she was a child. Something she didn't want anyone to know about."

"And it didn't say what it was?"

"No," replied Phoenix. "Just that it had been her fault. And that she had never been able to forgive herself for it."

Rose's eyes widened.

"Have you tried to find out what this terrible thing was?"

Phoenix shook his head. "I haven't had the chance," he said. "I promised myself I would, of course. I was planning on searching the house, in case something had been left lying around. And I thought I'd ask a few questions down in the village too. See if there was anyone there who remembered that far back. But then I lost the angel on our first day here, and I haven't got round to doing anything except look for that. I feel so terrible about losing it. It's the last connection I've got with my mum."

Rose brushed the sleet off the face of her torch.

"You must really miss her," she said.

Phoenix looked away.

"I'm all right," he muttered. "I'd rather not talk about it, actually. It's kind of easier that way."

For a time neither of them spoke.

"I suppose your dad doesn't know about you reading this letter?" said Rose at last.

"No," said Phoenix, "he doesn't. And he's not about to find out, either."

Rose glared at him. "Oh, come on! I said I wouldn't say anything, didn't I? And do you really think I'm the type to tell tales?"

Phoenix bowed his head. "Of course not. I'm sorry. I didn't mean it to come out like that. Thanks for keeping quiet when you knew I'd been told not to come over here. And – and for rescuing me just now too. It was so hot down there. And it was getting really hard to breathe. I…"

He tailed off, shuddering at the memory.

"Don't worry about it," said Rose quickly. "I'm just glad I saw you out of the window, that's all." She flushed. "And it's me who should be saying sorry, in any case. For not letting you have the attic bedroom, I mean. If you'd told me it had been your mother's, I would have let you have it, no problem."

"Ah, but I didn't tell you, did I?" said Phoenix.

"I was way too busy keeping everything a secret."

He looked up.

"And since you mention it, of course I miss my mum. I miss her like mad. I know it sounds stupid, but sometimes it feels like I've lost part of myself – a leg or an arm or something…"

"I don't think it sounds stupid at all," said Rose. She held her cousin's gaze. "You've still got your dad, though, haven't you? I mean, I know he's always got his nose in a book and everything, but he tries his best."

Phoenix sighed. "I know he does. And I know I don't exactly make things easy for him either."

He gave the bolt a final polish and placed it back alongside its glowing twin.

"Strange, aren't they?" he said. "What d'you reckon they are?"

"I haven't a clue," said Rose. She reached out and touched the bolt she had brought with her from the house. "D'you think they're both from over here?"

"It would make sense, wouldn't it?" said Phoenix. "Though goodness knows why that one was hidden under a floorboard in the attic. Maybe it was my mum who put it there. Maybe it was another of her peculiar secrets."

He gathered up the bolts and hauled himself upright.

"Come on. Let's go back in case Dad wakes up and starts getting suspicious. I'm going to need a bath, I reckon."

Rose cast her eyes over her cousin's earth-caked clothes. "You'll be having it in the dark," she said, getting to her feet. "There's been a power cut over at the house."

"Why doesn't that surprise me?" grunted Phoenix. He stepped back from the burrow and turned to leave the mound. "What is it with this place?"

The next minute he was stumbling over something lying in the wet grass.

"My torch!" he cried, picking it up and giving it a shake. "So that's where it landed. And look, it still works!"

He shone it around, then gasped.

"What is it?" exclaimed Rose. "What's the matter?"

Phoenix cowered beside her.

"That's what's the matter," he said. "That – that *thing* over there…"

Rose frowned. "What thing?" she said. "All I can see is mist and sleet."

Phoenix spun round to face her. "You can't see it?"

Rose focused her own torch in the same place Phoenix had been pointing his.

"No," she said. "Whatever it is, I definitely can't

see it." She eyed her cousin. "Are you sure you're OK?"

"I'm fine," snapped Phoenix. "Totally fine. It's just…"

He broke off, twisting back to where he could see the pale shape now retreating into the darkness.

"Look," he said. "I wasn't going to tell you any of this. I thought you'd laugh at me. But you remember what you said earlier, about something freaking me out?"

Rose nodded.

"Well, you were right. Something *did* freak me out. A weird sort of silhouette thing. It's been on the mound every time I've come over. And it's here now, hovering just over there."

Rose glanced around her uneasily.

"Are you telling me you've seen some kind of *ghost*?" she said.

"I don't know," said Phoenix. "I suppose so. I…" He stared down at the ground. "You think I'm crazy, don't you? You don't believe in things like that?"

Rose sighed. "I'm not sure what I believe in right now. Let's face it, if you'd asked me yesterday how likely it was that I'd find a glowing bolt underneath the floorboards, I would have thought you'd gone mad. So who's to know what's possible?"

She started to make her way down the side of the mound.

"But one thing's for sure. The local people think this place is haunted. The mound especially. It says so in the guidebook I bought at the station."

"Haunted?" echoed Phoenix, hurrying to catch her up. "Haunted by what?"

His cousin shrugged.

"I don't know," she said. "But I think I know someone who might."

9.
THE GARBLINGS

Dr Wainwright looked up as Phoenix sidled into the kitchen.

"What time do you call this, then? You do realize it's gone ten o'clock?"

Phoenix sat down at the table and yawned.

"Sorry, Dad," he said, helping himself to a slice of bread. "I must have needed the sleep. But it doesn't matter, does it? We're not going anywhere today."

His father gave a long sigh.

"Actually," he said, "I'm afraid we are. I've reached the end of my patience with this house. Just as soon as Rose is up and we've all had breakfast, we're packing our bags and heading home."

Phoenix gaped at him, his hand halfway to the marmalade jar.

"But Dad, we *can't*!" he exclaimed. "We only got here on Sunday."

His father raised his eyebrows. "You've changed your tune, haven't you? It wasn't so long ago you were begging me not to bring you here at all." He shook his head. "This is no holiday, Phoenix. Surely you can see that? The weather's terrible. The house is a wreck. We've got no central heating or hot water, and now there isn't any electricity either. We can't even make toast this morning! As for you and Rose – well, I don't think I've heard you say one nice word to your poor cousin since she arrived. It doesn't exactly make for a great atmosphere."

Footsteps sounded in the hallway and the kitchen door opened.

"Hi there!" said Rose, coming round the table and drawing up a chair beside Phoenix. "Good night's sleep?"

Phoenix stifled a grin.

"Not bad," he said. "All things considered." His expression darkened. "Dad says he's had enough of this place and we're going to leave after breakfast. Tell him we can't, won't you? He's not listening to me."

"*Leave!*" exclaimed Rose. "But Uncle Joel, we can't possibly! There's loads of things Phoenix and I want to do down here. We haven't even started yet."

Her uncle stared at her. "I thought you two

weren't even talking to each other. I thought…"

He sat back in his chair.

"What's brought this on, then? Yesterday the pair of you were at daggers drawn."

Rose glanced across at Phoenix.

"He's not so bad really," she said. "He just takes a bit of getting used to, that's all."

Phoenix elbowed his cousin beneath the table – but he was smiling. "Oh, *charming*!" he said. "I could say the same about you!"

Dr Wainwright folded his arms.

"Well, well," he said. "Seems I spoke too soon. Can't remember when I last saw a smile like that on your face, Phoenix. The company must be doing you good."

He peered more closely at his son.

"You're looking a bit peaky, mind. And what's that all over your neck?"

Phoenix flushed. "It's nothing," he said. "Just a bit of dirt." He busied himself with his breakfast. "Please let us stay a while longer, Dad. *Please*."

Dr Wainwright considered for a moment.

"OK – OK," he said at last. "I suppose we could give it another few days, if you really think you can amuse yourselves in this weather, that is. I've still got a ton of work to catch up on, but if I can crack on with it today I should be able to spend some proper time with you tomorrow. Take you out to a few local attractions, maybe."

He got up from the table.

"So what are you going to do with yourselves, then?"

Phoenix eyed his cousin. "We thought we might cycle into the village. It'd be good to have a change of scene."

"*Cycle?*" echoed his father. "Have you looked outside this morning?"

Rose laughed. "We'll be fine, Uncle Joel, honestly," she said. "We've got our waterproofs. And besides, the weather seems to be completely different down in the village, doesn't it? You said so yourself. We'll probably find it's baking hot there."

Dr Wainwright grunted. "Damned place," he muttered, making for the door. "It's really starting to get on my nerves. I'm off to put on another jumper before I freeze to death. You two have fun, and I'll see you back here at lunchtime."

Phoenix waited until his father had left the room, then turned to Rose.

"Well go on, then," he said. "Hurry up with your breakfast. I want to get into the village as soon as possible."

Rose reached for the bread. "You're sure you don't want us to go out and look for your angel first?"

Phoenix shook his head. "No," he said. "That'll just have to wait for now. I want to find out about these rumours, Rose. I want to know why people say the mound's haunted."

A few minutes later they were pulling on their waterproofs and racing round the side of the house. They wheeled the bikes out of the shed and pedalled up the track through the driving sleet.

At the junction with the road they skidded to a halt.

"It's just like you said it would be!" exclaimed Phoenix. He peeled off his waterproof and shaded his eyes from the brilliant sunlight now streaming towards them. "Cold and miserable inside the grounds and boiling hot the minute you get out on to the road. How can something like that even be possible?"

Rose frowned. "Don't ask me," she said, tying her waterproof round her waist. "I don't understand it any better than you. Come on, let's get into the village."

They set off side by side along the deserted road.

"Tell me what it said in that guidebook again," panted Phoenix. "About the mound, I mean."

Rose strained against the pedals of her bike.

"Just that it's believed to date from Anglo-Saxon times," she said. "It's supposed to be an ancient burial site, apparently. I guess that's why they reckon it's haunted. Whole thing sounds pretty strange to me. But still…"

"And what about the old man you met on the train? The one we're going to look for now. What exactly did he say to you?"

"I can't remember *exactly*," replied Rose. "I wasn't taking him too seriously at the time. But like I told you last night, he definitely thought Gravenhunger Manor was a bit odd. And he warned me not to go anywhere near the mound."

"But didn't he say why?"

"No, Phoenix, he didn't! I've told you everything I can, OK? With any luck you'll be able to ask him yourself in a minute. It can't be more than a mile or so from here."

They cycled on in silence and it wasn't long before they were weaving their way through the outskirts of the village and up the crowded high street, past shops selling ice creams and inflatable dinghies and buckets and spades.

"Here we are," said Rose, braking at last beside a bench and jumping off her bike. "This is where I saw him."

She peered through the pub window, then checked her watch. "No one's in there yet. It's only quarter to eleven. We're going to have to sit down and wait for a bit."

"And what if he doesn't turn up?" said Phoenix. "What if it was just a fluke you saw him here before?"

Rose rolled her eyes at her cousin. "Look on the bright side, why don't you? He'll be here. You'll see."

Phoenix shrugged.

He leaned his bike up against the wall of the pub and glanced at the row of shops.

"I'm going to get a drink while we're waiting," he said. "D'you want one?"

Rose nodded. "Yes, please. I'll stay here with the bikes."

She settled herself down on the bench and watched as Phoenix disappeared into the newsagent's.

The next moment she was on her feet again.

Walking towards her along the high street was the old man, clutching a small tin of tobacco.

Rose hurried over.

"Excuse me!" she said. "You probably don't remember me, but—"

"Of course I remember you!" exclaimed the old man. "How could I possibly forget! You're the young lady who was on her way to the manor."

He shuffled up to the pub bench and sat down.

"How are you finding it, then? Nothing wrong, I take it?"

"There's nothing wrong at all," said Rose. "It's just

that my cousin and I need some information and, well, we were wondering if you might be able to help us." She looked down at him a little nervously. "You see, his family used to live at Gravenhunger Manor. That's why we're staying there this summer. And…"

But the old man had stopped listening.

He was gazing over her shoulder, to where Phoenix had just emerged from the newsagent's.

"Here he is now," said Rose, stepping forward and taking a can of drink from her cousin. "Phoenix! This is the gentleman I was telling you about. I said we'd find him, didn't I?"

"Phoenix, hey?" muttered the old man. He glanced back at Rose. "And you say this young man's family used to live at the manor?"

"His grandparents lived there," replied Rose. "And his mother."

The old man shook his head from side to side.

"Well, well!" he murmured. "Who would have guessed it, eh? And after all this time too."

He struggled to his feet and stretched out his hand towards Phoenix.

"Nice to meet you, young man. I'm Bert, by the way. Bert Riley. Has anyone ever told you that you look exactly like your mother?"

Phoenix stared at him. "Are you — are you telling me you knew her?" he stammered at last.

Mr Riley sat back down and took his pipe from his pocket.

"I didn't *know* her as such," he replied. "But I certainly met her. She would have been about the same age as you, I suppose. You're the spitting image of her, you really are."

He prised open the tin of tobacco.

"Tell me, how's she doing these days? Is she staying here too?"

There was an uncomfortable silence.

"She…" began Phoenix.

He looked down at the ground.

Rose cleared her throat. "Actually, we're here with Phoenix's father. His mother – my Aunt Elvira – died earlier this year."

Mr Riley frowned. "I'm sorry to hear that," he said. "I should have liked to have met her again. In happier circumstances, you understand."

Phoenix glanced up. "Happier circumstances?"

The old man began to fill his pipe. "I met your mother just the once, you see. I met her on the day it happened."

"On the day *what* happened?"

"The accident, of course."

"Accident? What accident?"

Mr Riley gawped at Phoenix. "You mean she never told you about it?"

Phoenix shook his head slowly, his eyes fixed upon the old man.

"I didn't even know Gravenhunger Manor existed until a couple of days ago," he said. "It seems – well, it seems my mum had a few secrets from me and my dad. Can you tell me what happened, please? I want to know. I *need* to know."

Mr Riley lit his pipe and leaned back against the bench. "Secrets, eh?" he murmured. "Dangerous things, in my opinion. Always come out in the end, one way or another." He gestured to Phoenix and Rose to sit down beside him.

"It was thirty years ago," he said. "Thirty years ago this spring. We'd just come back from the morning catch. Beautiful day it was. Calm sea. Blue sky. Not a bad haul either, if I remember rightly. Plenty of crabs and lobsters. We'd unloaded the boat and some of us had decided to head to the café for breakfast. It was then that we saw the crowd outside the police station. Half the village was there. We asked what was going on and they told us someone had gone missing up at the manor. A young boy."

"A *boy*?" echoed Phoenix.

Mr Riley nodded. "It was Lorenzo. Your mother's younger brother."

Phoenix froze. "But my mother didn't have a brother…"

"Oh yes, she did," said the old man briskly. "Six years old, he was. He and the rest of the family had moved in several weeks earlier. Not that we'd seen much of them, mind. Kept themselves to themselves. Weren't what you'd call the mixing type."

The colour had drained from Phoenix's face.

"Anyway, the police were putting together a search party and I offered to come along and lend a hand."

There was a pause while Mr Riley took a long draw of his pipe and blew out a perfect circle of smoke, which hung for a moment above their heads before disappearing to nothing.

"The first thing I noticed when we got to the manor was the weather. Remember what I said it was like that day down in the village? Cloudless blue sky and everything? Well, it wasn't like that up there. There'd been a storm earlier on, apparently, and though the worst of it had passed, it was still pouring with rain when we arrived. It was cold too. Most of us had come in our shirtsleeves, and it wasn't long before we were freezing half to death."

The old man gave a wry smile.

"Of course, these days Gravenhunger Manor is famous for its bad weather. There's always a blooming rain cloud hanging over the place. Mrs Pugh from the baker's used to go up there once in a while to keep an eye on it. Only person brave enough to do the job, but even she went armed with a brolly. More to ward off evil spirits than the rain, I reckon."

Phoenix and Rose exchanged glances.

"In any case, the parents were in the front room talking to the sergeant, and your mother – Elvira – was with them. All pale and frightened-looking, she was. She said that she and her brother had been playing a game of hide-and-seek inside the house. It had been Lorenzo's turn to hide, but after she'd finished counting she couldn't find him anywhere. She went to tell her mother and when *she* couldn't find the boy either she'd phoned her husband at work and the police had been called. They'd checked to see if any of his belongings had gone missing with him: his little red tricycle, his piggy bank, that sort of thing. And that's when they discovered his toy boat had disappeared. There was talk he might have disobeyed his parents and gone off to sail it by himself, though the river had already been checked several times and there was no sign of him down there."

Mr Riley shook his head gravely.

"The police decided we should split up and search everywhere again," he continued. "Some people were given the task of checking the house, while the rest of us went outside to scour the grounds. I was asked to cover the area beyond the river."

He sucked hard on his pipe.

"I didn't like doing it, of course. I didn't like doing it one bit. You can't live in Gravenhunger all your life without knowing that somewhere between the river and the sea stands the mound, and I didn't want to go anywhere near it. But those were my instructions, and I could scarcely let everyone down."

"But why were you so afraid to go near it?" asked Rose, one eye on Phoenix.

Mr Riley stared at her. "Because of the garblings, of course," he said.

"The garblings?"

"Village talk, young lady. Folklore. Legend. Call it what you will. Age-old tales warning the inhabitants of Gravenhunger to keep away from the ancient mound in the grounds of the manor."

"But *why*?" asked Phoenix.

"Everyone has their own story to tell," replied Mr Riley, shrugging. "There's tales of hundreds of men swarming around up there in days gone by, shouting and singing and carrying fiery torches. There's some say there's treasure buried beneath the mound. Others who claim it's a burial ground. But whoever you listen to, there's one thing they all agree on."

"And – and what's that?"

Mr Riley leaned forward.

"It's cursed, young man. Haunted. It's not a place

to be, all right? Not a place to meddle with."

He narrowed his eyes at Phoenix.

"And it's definitely not a place for children."

"So what happened when you reached the river?" asked Rose hurriedly. "Did you get to the other side?"

"I did indeed. The banks were swollen nearly to bursting, but there was a tree trunk lying across the river and—"

"You crossed via the tree-trunk bridge?" blurted out Phoenix. "It was there *then*?"

Mr Riley spluttered on his pipe.

"I *knew* it!" he exclaimed. "You've been over there, haven't you? You've been on the mound! In spite of everything I told your cousin at the railway station? In spite of my warnings? You're playing with fire, young man. Just look where it got your mother, eh?"

"What do you mean?" asked Phoenix.

Mr Riley looked at him darkly. He ran his finger slowly round the bowl of the pipe. "It's my guess," he said, "that somebody triggered the curse that day. Went over to the mound and disturbed it in some way. And I reckon that somebody was your mother."

He raised his hand before Phoenix could interrupt.

"Of course, I've no actual proof. By the time I got up there the place had been ravaged by the storm. Any evidence would have been washed away completely by the rain. But something odd was going on: the freak weather, the unexplained disappearance of the little boy. And there was something in the way your mother…"

He broke off, frowning.

"Go on," urged Phoenix.

"Well, when I came back from my search, young Elvira was standing by the swings at the end of the garden. It was almost as if she'd been waiting for me. Keeping an eye on me, even."

"And – and what did she say to you?"

"Nothing," said Mr Riley. "Nothing at all. She looked at me for a split second and then she turned on her heel and ran back to the house. But in that moment I could tell she knew more than she was letting on. That girl was frightened. And not just frightened for her little brother either – frightened for herself."

He pursed his lips.

"There's no other explanation I can think of. Your mother must have been messing about on the mound – and who knows what trouble she'd stirred up by being there."

There was a long silence.

"I take it you never found Lorenzo?" murmured Phoenix.

Mr Riley shook his head. "We searched for the rest of the day, calling to each other through the mist and the rain to keep on looking and not to give up. When it grew dark some of us even went back to the village for torches and searchlights. But we didn't find him, and though most of us agreed he must have drowned in the river, no one ever truly knew what became of him." He sighed. "It was a dreadful day, a truly dreadful day. And one I have never been able to forget."

Beside him, Rose shifted on the bench, and glancing towards her, Phoenix could see that her eyes were full of tears.

"In memory of our angel," she whispered. "Lost but not forgotten."

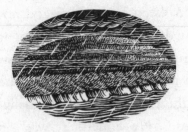

10.
THE PUZZLE

Elvira Phoenix pushed back her shock of jet-black hair and pressed her face against the attic window.

She sighed to herself. Three weeks at the new house, three weeks of perfect springtime exploring weather, and still she hadn't been past the end of the garden.

She had climbed the apple tree about a hundred times … swung on the swings Dad had hung from its branches until she felt quite dizzy … built dens in the rhododendron bushes … and lit campfires in the space between the fruit cage and the vegetable beds. She had done everything she could possibly think of – and now she was ready for something different. Before she started at her new school next week, she wanted a proper adventure.

Her eyes lingered over the weird-shaped mound beyond the pine forest.

Exactly what it was doing there she hadn't a clue. But since finding that book about the area yesterday afternoon, one thing was clear: she had to go and explore it.

She had discovered the book in the drawing room, high up on a dusty shelf – an ancient thing bound in dark red leather. On the front, in faded gold lettering, were the words "A Short History of Gravenhunger". It was mostly just a catalogue of boring facts, but at the back there were some black-and-white photographs, including a fuzzy snapshot of the very same mound she had been staring at from her bedroom window since the day they had arrived, and underneath it the line: Gravenhunger Mound: Anglo-Saxon burial site – rumoured to contain treasure.

She'd pleaded and pleaded to be allowed over there, but her parents had flatly refused. She wasn't to go further than the garden, they said. A deep river ran at the bottom of the forest, and there was no way she was going near it on her own. They'd take a look together when things were less busy, maybe. When they'd settled in at the manor and sorted themselves out a bit.

Elvira turned from the window.

If they weren't going to give her permission, then perhaps she should just do it anyway.

She was almost thirteen, for goodness' sake.

Really, what was the worst that could happen?

The door to the pub swung open and the landlord stepped out on to the pavement beside them.

"Morning, Bert!" he said, stooping to wedge open the door with a crate of empty bottles. "You're early this morning. And who's this you've got with you? I hope you haven't been stuffing their heads with silly nonsense."

Mr Riley knocked out his pipe on the arm of the bench. "I'll have you know I've been giving these youngsters some timely advice," he said. "Telling them some local history."

The landlord laughed.

"Don't you take anything our Bert says too seriously," he said, winking at Rose and Phoenix. "He's got that many stories in him you could fill a book."

Mr Riley sniffed and pulled himself to his feet. "I'm going inside," he said. "I daresay I'll see the pair of you around the village again."

He glared down at Phoenix. "That's if you stop your meddling, I might."

Phoenix flushed.

He watched as the old man followed the landlord into the pub, then leaned forward and put his head in his hands.

"Are you OK?" asked Rose.

"Oh yeah, I'm terrific," mumbled Phoenix. "It's a lot to get my head around, you know. It's not every day you find out your mother had a brother who vanished into thin air."

He straightened up and opened his can of drink.

"Lorenzo would have been my *uncle*, Rose. It's such a weird thought."

"I'm not exactly finding it easy to take in myself," said Rose, reaching for her drink. "Still, at least we're getting some answers now, aren't we? At least we know what the terrible thing was that happened down here."

Phoenix grunted. "It's about the only thing we *do* know," he said. "I mean, what about everything else Mr Riley told us? Honestly, I feel like someone's come along and totally scrambled my brain."

"This garblings business can't be more than silly rumour, surely," replied Rose. "Just being on the mound can't cause bad things to happen. It's impossible."

"As impossible as the silhouette I saw last night?" murmured Phoenix. "As impossible as the terrible weather and the glowing bolts?" He sighed. "I don't know what to make of it, really I don't. But you've got to admit it looks like my mother went over to the mound at *some* point. Think about the bolt you found underneath the floorboard. It's too much of a coincidence."

He gathered up their empty cans and threw them in a nearby bin.

"The point is, she obviously felt responsible for Lorenzo's disappearance. I told you what she wrote in the letter to Dad, didn't I? About the terrible thing being every bit her fault? About her never forgiving herself? I think Mr Riley's right, Rose. *Something* happened that day. Something which involved my mother and the mound and Lorenzo too. The question is, what?"

They mounted their bikes and began to make their way back down the high street.

"What were you muttering about earlier, by the way?" asked Phoenix, when at last they had left the village and were cycling along the road towards the manor. "Before the landlord came out of the pub, I mean? Something about an angel?"

"It was on an inscription I read. Inside the chapel at the manor," replied Rose.

"Chapel? What chapel?"

"You mean you haven't seen it?" exclaimed Rose. "It's tucked away in the forest at the side of the house. I came across it yesterday afternoon."

She shuddered. "Anyway, there was this plaque on the wall. It didn't have any dates on it, but it seemed quite new compared with all the other ancient stuff. On it were the words, 'In memory of our angel, lost but not forgotten'. I was thinking that maybe, well, that maybe it was put up for…"

"For Lorenzo?" said Phoenix.

Rose nodded.

There was a moment's silence.

"Why *angel*, though?" said Phoenix. "D'you think…"

He broke off.

"What?" asked Rose.

"No," said Phoenix. "It's nothing. It just seems a bit of a coincidence that the keepsake Mum gave me before she died was an angel, that's all. I was wondering if there might be some sort of a connection there."

They rounded the final corner to the manor and braked sharply.

Ahead of them, Dr Wainwright's car was parked up against the verge at the junction between the road and the track. Dr Wainwright was standing beside it, staring up at the sky.

"Dad?" called Phoenix, pedalling towards him. "Dad! Is everything all right?"

His father spun round.

"Ah," he said. "You're back. Well, I suppose that's one good thing at least."

"What's up?" said Phoenix. "What are you doing out here? I thought you were working this morning."

"I tried to," replied his father, "but I couldn't concentrate. It's too damned cold in that house to concentrate on anything."

He scowled down the track at the swirling rain and sleet.

"In any case, the weather seemed to have taken a turn for the worse and I thought I'd better come into the village and give you a lift back. I reckoned we could leave your bikes somewhere and pick them up later. And then," Dr Wainwright continued, "I get to the end of the track and find *this*."

He turned towards the road again and looked up.

"A perfect summer's day! Bright blue sky and temperatures off the scale. Just as it was when I went out yesterday. Just as it was the day we arrived, for that matter. There's no logic to it at all – it's almost as if the place is cursed."

Phoenix glanced across at Rose, but said nothing.

"I'm sorry, kids. I know I said I'd give it a few more days, but I really don't want to stay a moment longer."

"But—"

Dr Wainwright held up his hand.

"No arguments, Phoenix. We're leaving. There's something not right here. I can't put my finger on what it is exactly, but I'm afraid I don't like this place one bit."

He climbed back into the car and wound down the window.

"I'm going into the village to fill up with petrol

and get a few snacks for the journey. Can you two start packing? We can call your parents when we're on our way, Rose."

Phoenix and Rose watched as the car pulled off the verge and disappeared in the direction of the village.

The next minute Phoenix had kicked off from the tarmac and was speeding down the track through the wall of sleet.

"Wait for me!" shouted Rose, tugging on her waterproof and pedalling furiously to catch up with him. "*Phoenix! Wait for me!*"

Phoenix reached the driveway, then jumped off his bike and started to sprint towards the garden.

"Where are you going?" yelled Rose. She threw her bike down beside her cousin's and chased after him. "You heard what your dad said! We've got to go and pack!"

At the bottom of the garden Phoenix twisted round to face her.

"Isn't it obvious where I'm going?" he said. "I've got to go back to the mound. I've got to see if there's something I've missed. Something that might help explain all this. I need to know, Rose. I need to understand what happened that day."

He turned back towards the pine trees and plunged into the darkness.

Rose stood there for a moment, her hair white with the falling sleet.

And then she followed him into the forest.

Elvira darted between the pines.

She'd done it! She'd actually done it! She'd made it out of the house and into the forest without being seen. At the last minute she had even managed to slip into the garden shed and help herself to a little trowel that she could use for digging into the mound. After all, who knew what treasure she might find beneath it?

The trees were thinning out now, and ahead of her she could hear the sound of the river running not far off.

It was louder than she had imagined. Quite a lot louder, in fact. And as she threaded her way through the remaining pines, she suddenly saw why.

The snatches of blue ribbon she had glimpsed from the attic window had been only fragments of a massive whole. Close up the river was as wide as it was deep, and it was moving fast too. Beneath the sunlight that danced on its surface lurked currents which would surely drag her under in seconds.

Elvira's heart plummeted.

There was no way she could swim across this. Even on a beautiful spring day like today, with the sky the colour of a thrush's egg and nothing but the gentlest of breezes to ruffle the water, it would be crazy.

Suddenly her eye was caught by something dark straddling the river a little further downstream. She started towards it, her legs brushing against the nettles and brambles.

Now she could see it – a vast uprooted pine tree, its trunk stretching all the way from the edge of the forest to the opposite bank of the river.

Elvira quickened her pace, a smile spreading on her lips.

It looked like getting to the other side wasn't going to be so hard after all.

Phoenix reached the top of the mound and paused to catch his breath.

He saw it almost at once, drifting amidst the sleet not far from where he was standing – the same silhouette he had seen the previous day, but clearer now and more defined.

His skin prickled against his clothes. Was he dreaming, or was that the faintest outline of a hand he could see … a web of trailing fingers amidst the haze of greyish-white?

Rose appeared over the crest of the mound, red-faced from running after her cousin.

"What is it?" she asked. "Can you see that thing again? Is it still here?"

Phoenix nodded.

He glanced back to where the shape was now moving off towards the other side of the mound.

"It's weird," he said, pulling on his waterproof and zipping it up. "It's like it knows when someone else is with me. It's as if … it's as if it's only here for me."

Rose considered for a moment. "Perhaps that's not so surprising," she said. "After all, you're the one with the connection to this place, aren't you? You're the one whose family owns Gravenhunger Manor."

She gazed around.

"So what do we do now, then? What's the plan?"

Phoenix looked at her.

"Well, we think it's likely Mum found the bolt on the mound, don't we?" he said. "But maybe she just stumbled across it by accident. Maybe she was really looking for something else."

"Like what?"

"I don't know. Treasure, maybe? She might not have heard the local gossip like we have, but that wouldn't have stopped her from wondering what might lie beneath such a strange hump of ground."

"I suppose not," agreed Rose.

Phoenix crossed to the centre of the mound and knelt down.

"I need to put myself in Mum's shoes. I need to imagine I was her that day."

He began to scratch away the surface covering of sandy soil.

"And if I was looking for treasure, I reckon I'd start here – right in the middle."

11.
THE WHISPER
INSIDE THE EARTH

The view from up here was incredible.

She could see for miles around – right out to sea in one direction and over the chimneys of Gravenhunger Manor in the other. It was like being on top of the world.

Elvira wiped the sweat from her forehead and crouched back over the hole she was digging in the mound.

It was getting quite deep now, but so far she had found nothing. There was a steady thickening of the soil as she dug deeper, but that was all.

She wasn't ready to give up yet though. Not when there might be real treasure to find. And anyway, being over here on her own was way better than hanging around the house and garden all day looking after Lorenzo. If she had to play one more game of hide-and-seek with him she'd go mad. Little brothers could be such a nuisance.

The trowel struck something hard and Elvira's heart soared.

Throwing it to one side, she reached into the earth with her hands. There it was: a stub of metal, not much longer than her finger, but thicker and pitted all over. A piece of bronze, perhaps? A lump of gold studded with jewels?

She loosened the object from the soil and drew it out, her pulse racing.

But even before she had rubbed it clean, she could see that what she had found was nothing special.

It was just a rusty iron bolt.

Elvira dropped it back into the hole and sighed.

If there was anything interesting to discover beneath this mound, then she obviously wasn't looking in the right place.

She checked her watch. Five o'clock already! Dad would be home from work soon. She was going to have to get back to the house double-quick and clean herself up.

Tomorrow, if she got the chance, she would slip out again and dig some more — maybe in the middle this time. That would make much more sense, wouldn't it?

Nudging the trowel into the hole, she glanced down once more at the iron bolt, then reached inside and picked it up.

Perhaps she would take it with her after all.

It might not be treasure, but it could be the beginning of her collection, couldn't it?

She pushed it into her jeans pocket and stood up.

And above her, the April sky grew suddenly dark.

"This is ridiculous," said Rose. "Just look at the state of our hands! They're all blistered and scratched." She got to her feet, blinking the sleet out of her eyes. "I'm going back to the house to find something to dig with. There might be a spade in the shed."

Phoenix looked up at her and shrugged. "Suit yourself. But I'm staying here. We haven't got much time."

He glanced across at the silhouette, then forced his gaze away and watched as Rose disappeared down the side of the mound.

They'd been scrabbling away for nearly twenty minutes now and had made very little headway. The hole wasn't very deep at all, and their fingers were red-raw where they had snagged against stones and twigs hidden beneath the sandy soil.

He clawed his hand once more into the earth, Mr Riley's words reverberating inside his head.

There's some say there's treasure buried beneath the mound...

Was that really what his mother had been hoping to find?

If so, what had happened to her over here? And how could it possibly have had anything to do with Lorenzo's disappearance?

Phoenix swallowed.

Just the thought of the little boy's name made his blood run cold. His mother had had a brother, and he had never known. Perhaps Dad hadn't known either.

He sighed, then caught his breath as his fingers scuffed against a hard, narrow ridge buried inside the earth.

Freeing it from the soil, he stared down at the jagged lump of metal in his hand.

For a moment confusion mingled with the sour taste of disappointment.

So much for treasure. It seemed he had uncovered nothing more exciting than the remains of a trowel, its wooden handle rotten and wasted.

And then it dawned on him.

Was it possible that he had truly struck lucky … that his mother really had dug into the mound right here … and that this rusty old bit of metal was the tool she had been digging with?

Phoenix plunged the blade of the trowel into the earth, a shiver coursing through him.

In which case, what was it doing buried beneath the earth?

Horizontal sheets of rain lashed against the attic window, rattling the glass in its casement.

Elvira twisted and turned on the crumpled sheets.

Tomorrow wouldn't be much fun, would it?

Not if she and Lorenzo were going to be stuck inside the house all day while Mum carried on with the unpacking. No trips out till it was done, she'd said. Not even to the village.

It looked like there'd been a power cut too. The light had suddenly gone out when she'd been reading before bedtime, and when she'd checked, the switch down by her tape deck wasn't working either. At this rate they wouldn't even have the television for company in the morning.

Shivering, she pulled the quilt up round her shoulders.

And on top of her chest of drawers, the rusty iron bolt she had brought back with her from the mound began to glow.

Since finding the trowel, Phoenix had made swift progress. The hole was now so deep he was going to have to get right inside it in order to reach the bottom.

He began to climb in – then scrambled out again, his pulse quickening at the prospect of crouching in the narrow shaft below.

He couldn't. He just couldn't. Not after his experience trapped in the burrow the previous night. He would have to wait until Rose got back. If she'd managed to find a spade in the shed then they could carry on digging from the surface. If not, his cousin would have to get inside the pit and take a turn at scooping out the earth herself. In the meantime, he would make things easier by widening the hole as best as he could from up here.

Phoenix bent back over the edge and scraped another trowelful of earth towards him, then gasped as a tiny bronze-coloured disc skittered down the side of the pit and landed with a clink at the bottom.

Sticking the trowel-stub into the soil behind him, he gazed into the hole, his eyes smarting at the blast of heat that had risen to greet him.

It was hard to see anything clearly in such a dark and confined space, but if he screwed up his eyes he could just make out a battered old coin, and beside it, a bright speck of blue.

Phoenix leaned forward and began to blow away the covering of hot dry soil, his heart thudding against his chest.

Clear of its dusty veil, the blue speck grew to the size of his fingernail before giving way to another speck, red this time.

Then came another … and another … a pattern of tiny blue and red stones, arranged in a perfect spiral and set into what appeared to be a thin plate of yellowish metal.

Now the plate was curving downwards … and Phoenix was straining towards it, gripping the side of the pit and blinking at what lay before him.

It was a shield, its centre studded with precious stones – real sapphires, real rubies – and set into nothing less than pure gold.

His fingertips brushed the sumptuous spiral of jewels.

And that was when he heard it.

A voice – little more than a whisper, yet impossible to ignore. A voice that seemed to be coming from inside the earth itself.

Elvira lined up the last of her brother's toy soldiers on the drawing-room floor and stood up.

"There you are," she said. "That's the whole army set up, Lorenzo. All ready for you to play with."

She dropped a kiss on top of his head. "I'll be back in a bit, OK? Then we can have a game of hide-and-seek before lunch."

Out in the hallway, she glanced into the kitchen. Mum was standing at the table with her back turned, surrounded by cardboard boxes and pieces of crumpled-up newspaper, humming to herself as she unpacked countless pieces of china.

Elvira tiptoed on towards the front door and opened it a crack.

It was pretty wild out there, and there was certainly no sign that the weather was about to improve. But it was only wind and rain – and it smelt wonderful, as if the whole earth had suddenly come alive.

She reached up and grabbed her anorak off the peg.

No one was likely to notice if she went out for a while, were they?

Stand up, boy, whispered the voice. *Stand up and look towards the river.*

Phoenix hauled himself back from the edge of the pit and got to his feet, the shield and coin already forgotten.

Exactly who was speaking to him and why didn't seem to matter. All he knew was that he had to obey the command.

He turned towards the river. Nearby he could see the silhouette hovering above the surface of the mound, its shimmering form suddenly restless and agitated … but now there was something else too. Something quite different. Burning through the sleet, a pillar of hazy light had appeared as if from nowhere and was shining down just in front of him.

The voice inside the earth whispered to him once more.

What can you see, boy? What can you see on the river?

Phoenix screwed up his eyes in an effort to catch a glimpse of the water far below, but the brightness had all but blinded him.

Come down, boy. Come down and see the riches of the past…

The light began to move off, dragging across the grass like a giant searchlight and drawing him with it down the side of the mound towards the river.

At the crest of the embankment it halted – and Phoenix with it.

He blinked back the brightness as the pillar of light set off once more and came to rest over the water.

Now he could hear the beating of drums … the clamour of voices … now he could see at last what he had been called to witness.

He scrambled down the embankment, hungry for what lay before him.

But even as he waded into the wild water and felt it sweep him from his feet, the pillar of light began to fade … and the magnificent spectre on the river vanished to nothing.

"Wait for me, Elvira! Wait for me!"

Elvira twisted round on the tree-trunk bridge, gusts of wind ruffling her short black hair.

Her brother was stumbling through the undergrowth towards her, dressed in only a thin blue cotton shirt and shorts and clutching his toy boat.

"What are you doing?" she cried. "You're supposed to be in the drawing room playing with your soldiers!"

"I don't want to play with my stupid soldiers!" Lorenzo shouted back. "I want to play with my boat. Daddy said we could go and sail it."

"He didn't mean today! Not with the river practically bursting its banks! He meant on a nice sunny day. And with him there to help you!"

Elvira narrowed her eyes at her little brother. "How did you know where to find me, anyway? You've not been over here before, have you?"

Lorenzo shook his head.

"I saw you digging on that hill thing yesterday," he said. "I watched you from your bedroom window. And then I saw you going outside just now and I thought you might be going back there."

"You saw me on the mound? You went into my room without my permission?"

"I just wanted to play with you."

He looked at her proudly.

"I found my way through the forest all by myself. I followed the path you'd made. I ran and ran to catch up with you."

Elvira sighed.

"Well, you're just going to have to run and run all the way back again then, aren't you?" she said. "You can't come over here. It's far too dangerous."

"I don't care," said Lorenzo. "I'm not going back to the house. It's boring there."

He gazed across the river at his sister.

"I want to come with you. Are you digging for treasure?"

"You heard what I said, Lorenzo! Go back to the house this minute!"

"I'll tell on you if you don't let me come. I'll tell Mum where you've been."

"You wouldn't dare…"

"Yes I would."

Elvira stared at her brother for a moment.

"Fine," she said at last. "If that's what you want. Stay right there, OK?"

She began to shimmy back along the upturned pine.

Lorenzo waited until his sister was safely across, then darted forward and pressed something into her hand.

"Hold on to my angel for me," he said. "I don't want to drop it in the water."

Elvira groaned.

"Do you really have to carry that thing around with you everywhere you go?" she said.

"Yes," replied Lorenzo. "Gran gave it to me. It's my most favourite present in the world. She says it reminded her of me."

"Some angel you are!" grunted Elvira. "Gran doesn't know you at all!"

She pushed the silver angel into her pocket, then helped her brother on to the huge pine and circled his waist with one arm.

"OK, you little pest, let's go. I'll be behind you all the way."

Rose burst out of the forest and hurried through the wind and sleet towards the tree-trunk bridge.

She had found nothing they could dig with in the shed – and quite honestly, she was glad. The moment she got back to the mound she was going to persuade Phoenix to see sense. It was time to stop messing about with something they didn't understand.

What did her cousin expect to gain by stirring up the past like this, anyway?

He was never going to find out exactly what had happened here thirty years ago. The only two people who knew that were both dead. And nothing he did now was going to change that.

In any case, her uncle would be back from the village soon and they needed to start packing. The last thing she wanted to do was get herself into a load of trouble.

Rose clambered on to the massive pine and began to shuffle towards the opposite bank.

Halfway across she stopped.

On the other side of the river, a little way downstream, a dark head was bobbing about in the racing water…

"*Phoenix!*" she screamed. "*Phoenix! What d'you think you're doing?*"

The head twisted round and a pair of terrified eyes stared briefly back at her before disappearing beneath the foamy scum of the river.

A few seconds later her cousin resurfaced, but even further downstream now, towed ever seaward by some vicious, invisible current.

Rose cast about her wildly for something she could throw him … something she could use to pull him out of the water. A rope would do it … a rope was what she needed, and she'd seen one only a few minutes ago in the shed. But there was no time to go back to the house now. Phoenix wasn't going to last that long.

She kicked out against one of the remaining side branches of the pine as it chaffed against her leg, then bent down and grabbed hold of it.

Wrenching it free from the trunk, she hauled herself along the bridge, one hand clinging to the slippery bark, the other wielding the shorn-off branch.

"*Hang on in there, Phoenix! Hang on in there! I'm coming!*"

She jumped down on to the bank and blundered through the undergrowth.

"*Get a hold of this!*" she shouted. She sprawled on the ground and thrust the branch over the furious river. "*Grab it and I'll pull you out!*"

Phoenix floundered towards it, his skin blue with cold.

Twice he nearly grasped it – and twice the water flung him back, eddying and swirling around him in a grey-green maelstrom of froth and spume.

Rose clung to the edge of the bank.

Something lodged inside it was digging into her palm, but she ignored the pain, stretching further and further over the river in an effort to reach her cousin.

Once again he lunged for the branch – and this time his fingers grazed its tip.

"*That's it, Phoenix! Just a little bit further…*"

One final lurch and he had it in his grip, relief flooding his face.

Prising her hand from the bank, Rose fed the branch back towards her, sensing the weight of her cousin against the pull of the river.

When at last he was close enough, she reached down and dragged him out of the water.

"*What were you playing at?*" she cried. "I leave you alone for five minutes and come back to find you drowning in the river…"

Phoenix said nothing.

He lay there in the undergrowth, shivering and panting ... and it was only then, glancing down at her throbbing hand, that Rose saw the marks in her skin.

Whatever was wedged into the bank had punctured her flesh in several places: three holes had been pierced at regular intervals across her palm.

She wiped away the blood and leaned back over the side of the river to see what had caused such deep wounds.

Something was poking out of the mud ... something crafted from wood and studded all over with tiny, rusted nails.

Working it free, Rose pulled it out.

In her hand, caked in mud but still perfectly recognizable, was a small toy boat.

12.
THE NAIL HEADS

"I don't like it here," said Lorenzo. He glanced up at the blackening sky. "I want to go home. I feel all cold and shivery."

Elvira twisted round from the hole she was digging in the centre of the mound.

"I'm not surprised you're cold," she said. "You've hardly done any digging, have you? And I thought you wanted to help."

Lorenzo scuffed at the ground with his shoes.

"That's because there's nothing to find," he grumbled. "It's just a stupid hump of earth, that's all."

His sister sighed. "Perhaps you're right," she said. "But until we've dug a bit deeper we won't know for certain, will we? Who knows — we might be really close to discovering some priceless piece of treasure."

She peeled off her anorak and threw it to her brother.

"Here. Put this on. It should keep off some of the rain, at least."

Lorenzo struggled into the anorak and for a few moments there was silence, save for the buffeting of the wind and the rain and the soft scrape of metal against earth.

"Elvira?"

"What is it now?"

"Can we go and sail my boat on the river? I'm sure we can find a bit that isn't too deep."

"No!" snapped Elvira. "We can't! I've told you, it's far too dangerous down there." She sank her trowel once more into the sandy soil. "You've got to be a big boy and keep your side of the bargain, OK? You've got to wait until I'm done."

"But—"

"Oh, for heaven's sake, Lorenzo! Leave me alone and stop whingeing, will you? You're driving me mad!"

Lorenzo scowled.

He snatched up his toy boat and started to walk away, dodging a trowelful of earth that his sister had just flung over her shoulder.

As it landed on the growing pile beside the hole, something caught his eye. In amongst the soil and stones was a small circle of bronze-coloured metal, not much bigger than a thumbnail.

Bending down, he picked it up and polished it on his shorts.

It looked like money. A bit different from the coins he kept in his piggy bank – smaller and thinner and sort of wobbly round the edges – but money all the same. It was strange, though. The object in his hand felt warm, almost as if it were alive.

He opened his mouth to call to his sister – then stopped.

A column of milky light had appeared in front of him, and a whispered voice was calling to him from inside the earth ... a voice he had never heard before.

Lorenzo looked up into the light, listening to what the voice was telling him and smiling at the unexpected warmth on his upturned face.

The coin slid from his grasp back on to the heap of discarded soil.

And still clutching his toy boat, he began to walk towards the river.

Phoenix propped himself up against the riverbank and took the little boat from Rose.

He scraped off the lumps of earth that clung to its sides and rubbed it on his soaking jeans.

The frame was rotten in places and some of the nails that held it together had worked themselves loose, but the basic shape was clear enough – an open wooden shell, flattened at its base, each end arched upwards in a graceful point.

"D'you think it's his?" whispered Rose, hugging herself against the cold.

Phoenix nodded. "It must be. It all fits, doesn't it?"

"So you reckon what Mr Riley said was right, then? That Lorenzo drowned in the river? Oh, Phoenix. I can't bear it. It's too horrible to imagine…"

"Maybe he followed my mum through the forest when she came over to the mound," said Phoenix. "Maybe he was hoping to sail his boat."

Rose looked at her cousin. "You think he tried to cross the tree-trunk bridge by himself and fell into the river?"

Phoenix considered for a moment.

"I suppose it's possible," he said. "But Mum must have been involved in some way, surely? Why else would she have felt so guilty? I reckon it's more likely the pair of them went across the bridge together and made it as far as the mound."

He cradled the toy boat in his hands.

"Perhaps she persuaded him to wait for her while she dug. And perhaps he had a bit of a dig around himself. Yes … yes … that would definitely make sense."

"If you say so," muttered Rose. "It doesn't make much sense to me."

She frowned. "So you think he just got bored and wandered off by himself, do you? And that's when the accident happened?"

Phoenix shook his head.

"No," he said, "I don't. I know this sounds ridiculous, but I think he touched something he shouldn't have done. And because of that he got drawn towards the river." He glanced away, flushing. "Exactly the same way I got drawn towards it just now."

Rose gaped at her cousin. "You're saying you were *led* down here?"

Phoenix stared at the little boat and ran his fingers over the nail heads that studded its sides.

He thought back to what the whispering voice had said to him.

Come down, boy. Come down and see the riches of the past…

"Just after you left me I found an old trowel in the hole we were digging," he explained. "I'm pretty sure it was what my mother had been using. And when I dug down further I uncovered a bronze coin and a shield studded all over with jewels."

Rose's eyes widened.

"I reached out to touch them," Phoenix continued, "and the next thing I knew there was this weird light shining in front of me and a voice from the earth calling me down to the river. And when I got there I saw…"

He broke off, his fingers clenched round the toy boat.

"You saw what?" breathed Rose.

Phoenix said nothing.

His fingers were moving again, running backwards and forwards over the nail heads as if they were measuring the distance between each tiny point of metal.

"Come on, Phoenix! Tell me what you—"

"We've got to get back to the mound," interrupted Phoenix, his eyes flashing with excitement. He started to haul himself up from the riverbank. "Now."

"But we can't!" exclaimed Rose. "You're dripping wet! You'll freeze to death if you stay out here much longer. And anyway, Mr Riley was right, can't you see? The garblings aren't just empty rumour after all. There really is something strange about the mound. I mean, look at what's just happened to you. You might not be so lucky next time."

She reached out towards him, but Phoenix pulled away.

Already he was making for the embankment, Lorenzo's little boat in his hand.

"I have to go back there one more time, Rose. I have to. You see, I think I know what's underneath it."

152

Elvira jumped as a clap of thunder sounded overhead.

"Time to go back, Lorenzo," she muttered. "Looks like there's a proper storm brewing."

Leaving the trowel at the edge of the pit, she straightened up.

"Lorenzo? Did you hear me?"

She looked around her.

Her brother was nowhere to be seen ... and nor was his toy boat.

Elvira rushed over to the side of the mound, a cold sickness rising up from the pit of her stomach.

Surely he hadn't gone off to sail it without her? Not with the river as it was...

"Lorenzo!" she shouted. "Lo-ren-zo!"

She raced towards the river, still crying out his name.

Perhaps he'd got bored with waiting and decided to go back to the house to dry off.

But that would mean crossing the tree-trunk bridge all by himself ... and he couldn't swim...

At the crest of the embankment she skidded to a halt, forcing her eyes downwards to scan the furious watery spew of greys and greens and dirty whites, but there was no sign of her brother.

Was it possible he had made it across OK after all? Might he already be safely home?

Elvira scrambled down the embankment and hurried over to the tree-trunk bridge.

If she had been just a few moments earlier, she might have caught sight of her own blue anorak ... scudding down the surface of the river towards the sea beyond.

"Talk to me!" shouted Rose, struggling to catch up with Phoenix as he approached the mound. "Tell me what's going on!"

She hurried up the slope after him, her shoulders hunched against the driving sleet.

"You still haven't told me what you saw when the voice drew you towards the river. Was it some sort of a *vision* you were having?"

Phoenix didn't answer.

He clambered to the top, then stopped abruptly.

"What's the matter?" asked Rose, hauling herself up the last stretch. "Oh, come on, Phoenix. Don't tell me you're still surprised to see that silhouette thing hanging around up here." She came to stand beside him, panting. "I told you, it's—"

"No," interrupted Phoenix. "It's not the silhouette. I mean, I can see it and everything. But it's not that." He leaned his head to one side. "Listen, Rose. Stop talking for a moment and listen."

A low rumbling was coming from deep beneath them ... and round the edge of the mound a series of tiny hollows was starting to sink into the ground.

"What's happening?" cried Rose.

Beside her, Phoenix was standing very still, his eyes glued to the trembling earth.

He pointed towards the hollows.

"They're making a pattern, see? There ... and there ... and there ... a sort of stretched-out oval shape."

Rose stared about her.

The mound was a mass of hollows, stretching all the way round its summit and meeting in a tip at each end, the pattern interrupted only by the burrow Phoenix had fallen into the previous night.

She grabbed her cousin's arm.

"I don't like this," she said. "It's as if someone doesn't want us here. Let's get out of—"

Phoenix held up his hand to silence her.

"Wait!" he said. "We'll go in a minute, I promise. But first I need to show you something."

"*Phoenix...*"

"Watch me, Rose. Just watch me..."

Edging towards the nearby burrow, Phoenix pulled one of the glowing iron bolts out of his jeans pocket and dropped it neatly inside.

"Yeah?" said Rose. "So you've put it back in the burrow. So what?"

The rumbling seemed to subside a little as Phoenix rejoined his cousin and thrust Lorenzo's toy boat into her hands.

"Now hold this out in front of you," he instructed, wrenching his eyes away from the silhouette, which was darting backwards and forwards over the surface of the mound. "Hold it in one hand and give me the other."

Rose allowed him to take her free hand. She felt the rough arc of nails beneath her skin as Phoenix placed her fingertip on to a protruding nail head at one end of the boat and guided it across its length.

Lifting her finger off, he repositioned it on to the nail head directly below.

"For goodness' sake, Phoenix. We haven't got time for all this…"

But again her cousin was running the tip of her finger across the length of the boat … and again she could sense the bumpy pattern of tiny metal points.

"Got the shape?" said Phoenix, releasing her hand at last. "Feel the pattern?"

"Of course," said Rose. "It's how a boat's made, isn't it? Runs of rivets holding all the wooden planks together. It's not exactly rocket science." She glared at her cousin. "Come on, Phoenix! Stop talking in riddles. What are you trying to show me?"

"Can't you see?" said Phoenix.

He pointed his finger at the burrow, then moved his hand slowly all the way round the stretched-out oval of hollows.

Rose's eyes widened.

"Are you saying…?" she started.

And now her gaze was flitting between the toy in her hand and the pattern sunk into the still-shuddering earth.

"Are you saying there's a *boat* underneath this mound?"

Elvira stood in the hallway and listened.

Whatever she'd been expecting, it hadn't been this.

At first she'd been pretty sure she would catch up with Lorenzo in the forest, and when she hadn't she had tried to persuade herself she would find him in the kitchen telling everything to Mum. There would be raised voices and slammed doors and a stinking great row.

But instead she had returned to an unnerving stillness.

Where, oh where, had her little brother got to? It just didn't make sense.

She had looked inside the kitchen already, but there was nobody in there. All the boxes had been cleared away and the cupboard doors were shut. Her mother must have moved on to tackle a different part of the house. The drawing room was empty too, save for the army of toy soldiers, all lined up and standing to attention – exactly as she had left them earlier.

Footsteps sounded directly above her head and Elvira's heart leaped. They were coming from Lorenzo's bedroom.

Perhaps he was up there after all, waiting for her to come and say she was sorry…

She sneaked up the stairs, but even before she had reached the landing she could see through the half-open doorway that it was only Mum in there, bent over yet another stack of cardboard boxes.

Elvira tiptoed past. She started to move up through the rest of the house – faster and faster now – checking inside every room as she went. Each time she opened a door her spirits surged … only to plummet seconds later.

On the fourth-floor landing she stopped.

"Please be up there," she whispered to herself. "Please, Lorenzo. Please be sitting on my bed grinning that mischievous grin of yours. If you are, I'll never be cross with you again, I promise. I'll play with you for the rest of the day. I'll do whatever you want…"

She raced up the narrow staircase and pushed open the door.

The room was empty.

Hurrying over to the window, she checked outside, willing her brother to burst out of the forest and run across the garden towards her … but there was no one out there.

Elvira sank down on her bed, her head in her hands. This was ridiculous. It wasn't even as if Lorenzo was any good at hiding, was it? When they played hide-and-seek together she always knew exactly where to find him. But now it wasn't a game any more, now he was missing for real; it seemed he'd managed to vanish into thin air.

If only she could shout out his name – at least that way she might be able to quell some of her crippling fear. But if she did that, Mum would guess at once that something was wrong.

She jumped at the sound of her mother's voice calling from the bottom of the stairs.

"Elvira? Are you up there?"

Elvira sat very still on the bed.

"Yes, Mum!" she called back. "I'm here."

"Is everything all right? You've got Lorenzo with you, haven't you?"

"Everything's fine," Elvira heard herself reply – and now she'd told one lie she couldn't stop. "We – we were just about to play a game of hide-and-seek."

She stared down at her mud-streaked clothes, praying that her mother wouldn't come up.

"OK!" shouted her mother. "I'll just unpack a few more boxes and then we'll have lunch."

Elvira listened as her mother's footsteps moved off across the landing.

What on earth was she going to do now? After what she'd told Mum, she could scarcely come down to lunch without Lorenzo…

Standing up, she made for the door.

She had to get out there again. She had to find him. He might have got lost in the forest … or wandered out on to the road … or fallen over and hurt himself … the possibilities were endless.

She crept back down the stairs, feeling inside her pocket for her brother's silver angel.

It didn't seem right her having it now. It didn't belong to her. Wherever Lorenzo was, the angel should be with him.

Phoenix looked at Rose, his eyes bright.

"It's exactly what I'm saying," he said. "There's a longboat buried directly beneath us. Or at least the remains of one. The wooden frame will have rotted away by now, but the bolts that held it together are still there. I'll bet you anything you like there's one below every hollow."

He gestured over the trembling mound, pausing for a second at the place where the silhouette now hung motionless amidst the sleet.

"There'll be bolts everywhere, of course," he went on. "It's just the position of the topmost ones that have been revealed to us. The bolt I discovered in the burrow must originally have been much higher up – I suppose it got dislodged when whatever animal it was tunnelled into the earth."

Rose gazed around her.

"Are you absolutely sure about this?" she said.

"Of course I'm sure," replied Phoenix. "What else

could possibly create a shape like this? Besides, it's what I saw in my vision."

"You *saw* what's lying underneath the mound?"

Phoenix turned and stared through the sleet towards the river.

"It was incredible, Rose. So majestic. So *graceful*. The ends of the boat were curved upwards into points and the sides were packed with oarsmen. And in the middle…"

He swallowed, struggling to keep his voice steady.

"In the middle, raised up on a sort of square platform, was a king. A warrior-king. He must have been the one calling me down to the river. He was wearing a massive bronze helmet with a face-mask. And there was a hoard of treasure at his feet. Piles and piles of jewels and coins. And he had a shield at his side, studded with sapphires and rubies."

"The same as the one you uncovered in the pit?"

Phoenix nodded.

"I saw the whole thing, Rose. The boat. The king. The treasure. Everything. Just as it once was. And it's all right here, buried beneath the mound."

He made to move across the juddering surface towards the pit in the centre, but Rose yanked him back.

"Oh no, you don't!" she exclaimed. "That treasure's done more than enough damage already."

"I wasn't going to *touch* it … I was only going to have a quick look."

"Don't even think about it…"

Rose shook her head at her cousin, then frowned. "So you reckon the king was buried here along with the boat, do you?"

"Yes," replied Phoenix. "I suppose it must have been some sort of ancient custom. A way for a tribe to honour its leader when he died. They must have dragged the boat up from much further downstream, where the embankment isn't so steep."

He glanced back towards the pit.

"In any case, the voice that lured me into the river sounded like it was coming from inside the earth itself. It was as if somebody was actually down there."

"Which they were," said Rose. "Protecting their treasure. This king of yours must have put a curse on the mound before he died. So that anyone who touched what was rightfully his would come to harm."

She shuddered. "It really was all there in the village garblings, wasn't it? The curse … the treasure … the burial ground… Just imagine what a spectacle it must have been. All those men hauling the boat up from the river and covering it with earth. There would have been hundreds of them."

"It's about the only bit I *do* have to imagine

though," said Phoenix. "I saw that boat, Rose. I actually *saw* it."

Rose eyed him sharply. "Yes," she said, "and it nearly cost you your life." She bit her lip. "And what about Lorenzo? Have you thought about him? Like you said, he must have touched something he shouldn't have – something belonging to the king – and been drawn towards the river too. Except he wasn't quite as lucky as you, was he?"

Phoenix screwed his eyes up tight, then opened them wide, as if he was trying to shake away the memory of his vision.

"He must have done it when my mum's back was turned, mustn't he?" he said. "She can't have had a clue what was happening to him, otherwise she would have tried to stop him."

He stared at his cousin.

"Perhaps she *never* worked out that the mound was cursed. It would explain the letter, wouldn't it? About the whole thing being her fault. Perhaps…"

"Perhaps … perhaps…" said Rose. "It's all just guesswork, isn't it? We're never going to know exactly what happened that day."

She put a hand on his shoulder.

"Come on. We've got to get going. Your dad'll be back any minute and you're freezing cold. Besides, I don't like it over here."

"But—"

"Look," Rose interrupted, "you've found out as much as you possibly can about your mother's secret. You've got to stop now, Phoenix. It's time to put the past back where it belongs."

Phoenix sighed. He turned and started to follow his cousin down the side of the quivering mound.

She was right, of course. If he didn't stop going over everything in his mind like this, he'd drive himself crazy. He really did have to try and put it all behind him.

He trudged down the slope through the steadily worsening sleet.

If only he could have one last glance at that shield… True, he had seen it already, but it was so mixed up with the vision and everything that had happened since, he no longer had a clear picture of it in his head. And what if all the rumbling and settling of the earth had exposed something else too? The great bronze helmet with its face-mask, perhaps? Or some of the jewels he had seen at the feet of the warrior-king?

Surely it wouldn't hurt to have one final look? It wasn't as if he was going to touch anything. All he wanted was an image to take away with him, something he could carry around inside his mind for the rest of his life.

He hung back a little, allowing his cousin to reach the bottom first, then whipped round and began to scramble up the mound once more.

"Phoenix!" yelled Rose. "*Phoenix!*"

She reached out towards him ... but it was too late.

A massive tremor was tearing through the earth beneath them, ripping Phoenix from his feet and catapulting him up into an explosion of fiery dust.

He landed just inches from where a jagged crack was snaking around the base of the mound, separating it from the grassy stretch of land beyond.

Staggering upright, he braced himself to jump across the gap, but already the two sides were wrenching apart and a chasm was opening up before him.

On the other side of the gulf, Rose was shouting to him ... jabbing her finger at the darkening air ... pointing behind him...

Phoenix glanced over his shoulder at the summit.

Cold fear flashed in his eyes.

High above him swirled a huge cloud of dust ... and something seemed to be sucking it down towards the very centre of the mound.

13.
THE EMPTY
HOLLOW

A scythe of electric-white light slashed across the sky, illuminating Elvira as she dashed between the pine trees.

She'd been this way already, surely? Perhaps she should try going in the opposite direction…

Twisting round, she stumbled over a hidden tree root and went crashing to the forest floor.

She lay there for a moment, her cheek pressed against the slimy layer of mud and pine needles, and then she began to sob.

It was no good. She would have to go back and tell Mum Lorenzo was missing. The grounds were just too huge to cover on her own — and in any case, it had been over half an hour since she had last seen her brother. There was no knowing where he might have got to.

But what was she going to say? As far as her mother was concerned they'd both been in the house playing hide-and-

seek. If she told the truth now, Mum would be livid. It looked like she would have to tell another lie to cover up the ones she'd already told...

Elvira got to her feet and set off back towards the manor.

She had nearly reached the border with the garden when she stopped.

What if Mum came down to the river to look for Lorenzo and saw the tree-trunk bridge? What if she went over to the mound and discovered the two holes? There'd be trouble then, for sure...

There was nothing else for it. Before she did anything else she was going to have to go and fill in those holes.

Elvira hurried back the way she had come. A few minutes later she was crossing the river and pulling herself up the embankment, blasts of cold rain whipping her face.

She raced towards the mound and scrambled up its windswept side, then rushed over to the pit in the middle and knelt down beside it.

She would start with this one ... and she would bury the trowel while she was at it. It wasn't as if she was planning on using it again, was it? Right now she'd be glad if she never came back here in her life.

Crooking her arm around the pile of soil heaped at its edge, Elvira began to draw it into the hole.

And in amongst the falling earth a small bronze coin went spinning to the bottom ... the same coin her brother had dropped only half an hour before.

Phoenix stood rooted to the spot.

It seemed there was nowhere to turn.

Above him twisted the vortex of descending dust and beneath him the gaping chasm stretched its ever-widening jaws.

He flinched as the remaining iron bolt seared through his jeans pocket into his thigh.

Cursing, he pulled it out.

What was happening to it? It had been warm before, but now it was burning hot – so hot he could hardly hold it.

Phoenix raised his arm, ready to hurl the bolt into the gulf below ... and then he lowered it, frowning.

From across the void Rose was screaming at him to lie down flat, to cling to the mound for all he was worth, but he took no notice.

What was it she had said to him at the top just now? Something about putting his mother's secret behind him? About putting it back where it belonged? Yes, that was it. *It's time to put the past back where it belongs.*

How could he have been so blind? He'd been holding on to the one thing he had needed all this time...

He turned to face the summit, brandishing the iron bolt above his head.

"So this is what you want, is it?" he yelled. "This is what you've been waiting for?"

He began to heave himself up the slope, his fingers curled around the bolt.

At the crest he paused.

The pit he had dug in the centre had become a churning mass, sucking everything in its path towards it: dust and stones, twigs and leaves. Now and then there was a flash of gold amongst the spinning debris … a gleam of silver … a sparkle of precious stone.

Phoenix gazed open-mouthed over the rest of the mound.

The whole surface was peppered with tiny hollows, no longer just round the edge but right across the top. The tremor seemed to have deepened them too … and nestled at the base of each one was a glowing iron bolt.

The earth gave another violent shudder and Phoenix was buffeted sideways.

"OK!" he shouted. "I know what I've got to do, all right? I know what I've got to find!"

He waited for the tremor to subside, then started to drag himself around the mound on all fours, the bolt burning in his hand.

And not far off, half hidden by the swirling dust, the silhouette darted to and fro over the luminous skeleton of the great boat.

Elvira huddled beneath the covers of her bed, her face wet with tears.

The police were still outside, along with some of the villagers who had come up to help. One or two of them had gone back for torches and searchlights and now they were scouring the garden yet again, calling to each other through the rainy darkness.

One man, whose job it had been to search beyond the river, had guessed she wasn't telling the truth, she just knew it. She had hung around at the bottom of the garden waiting for him to come back, dreading what he might have to say – and when at last he had emerged from the forest he had given her such a knowing look, as if he knew quite well that she had been over on the mound.

She hadn't wavered from her story, though. Lorenzo had grown tired of playing with his soldiers, she had said. She had agreed to play his favourite game of hide-and-seek, but when it had been his turn to hide, she hadn't been able to find him anywhere.

Elvira swallowed, remembering what had really happened ... the frantic searching of the house and grounds ... the race against time to fill in the two holes ... the sprint back to the manor ... the heart-stopping journey upstairs to wash and change into clean clothes ... the burying of the dirty ones at the bottom of the laundry basket in her room

... *and all the time, the only thing she could think of was Lorenzo. How she should never have allowed her brother to cross the river in the first place. How she shouldn't have let him out of her sight − not even for a second. How, if anything truly dreadful had happened to him, she would never forgive herself...*

It was then that she had spotted the iron bolt sitting on top of her chest of drawers. If anyone saw it, there would be questions. And besides, she never wanted to see it again. It was a reminder of just how stupid and selfish she had been.

She had snatched it up and pushed it under a loose floorboard beside the window, noticing neither its faint glow nor its warmth against the tingling of her freshly-scrubbed hands − and then she had raced downstairs to find her mother.

Mum had been pretty calm at first. She'd said Lorenzo was probably just playing a joke on them. But it wasn't long before she had started to panic too and Dad had been called back from work.

After that everything had happened very fast: the police had been summoned and a huge search party mounted. All day the house and its surroundings had hummed with activity.

Now though, things had quietened down. Most of the villagers had gone home, and whilst a few stragglers remained outside with the police, it was obvious from the sound of their voices that they no longer held out much hope.

Elvira burrowed further inside the bed.

If only she had been honest from the start, then maybe they might have had more chance of finding him ... if only she had told the truth when it had most mattered.

She reached up under her pillow and closed her fingers around the silver angel. If only ... if only...

There was no point wondering at what might have been – her little brother was gone.

And it was every bit her fault.

The tremors were getting closer and closer together.

He had twenty seconds at most ... twenty seconds to check inside as many hollows as possible before he would be forced to press himself to the ground, tensing his muscles against the juddering earth.

But how many more hollows were there?

Hundreds and hundreds of them ... too many to count ... yet he was going to have to look in every one.

Phoenix made to peer into the next hollow, his fingers clenched around the iron bolt, then cried out as another tremor, much stronger than anything that had come before, ripped through the earth, flinging him forward.

The next moment he was scrabbling against the blistering soil.

Something seemed to be pulling him towards the centre of the mound – an invisible force dragging him onward.

From all around he could hear the far-off clamour of voices mingling with the rhythmic beating of drums, and ahead of him the column of light had appeared once more, its milky rays illuminating the mouth of the ravenous pit.

Phoenix opened his mouth and screamed.

He knew how it would be down there: the heat … the lack of air … the impossible blackness. He had felt it all before. But now there was something worse than that – something far, far worse: the king himself.

Flailing out with his arms, he plunged the iron bolt into the earth.

At once he jolted to a halt.

He lay there, just inches from the rim of the pit, clinging to the bolt.

A terrible gleaming rose from within the hole … and he glanced down to see the great bronze helmet with its face-mask glaring up at him through the pillar of light.

Come on in, boy. Come and see the treasure for yourself.

Phoenix stared back into the empty eyes, his heart slamming against his chest.

Come on in. You know it's what you want…

For a moment it seemed that the eyes would suck

him in … that he was powerless to resist their magnetic pull…

"No!" he cried. "It's not what I want at all! Not any more!" He tore his gaze away. "You took Lorenzo, didn't you? You lured him into the river. Well, you're not having me too!"

He tightened his grip around the bolt.

If he could just use it to get back to the edge … to where he would be safe from the pull of the pit…

He wriggled back until he was at full stretch, then in one swift movement pulled out the bolt and rammed it into the earth in front of his chest.

Three times he dragged himself backwards … three times he repositioned the bolt … and then he stopped, spread-eagled over the surface of the mound.

Now he must wait … now he must hold firm until after the next tremor. There was no way he could risk being flung towards the pit again. He didn't have the strength to get himself back a second time.

He listened for the familiar rumbling of the earth, squeezing his eyes shut against the hot blanket of dust that was surely about to envelop him.

But it did not come.

Thirty seconds must have passed since the last tremor … forty … fifty … and all around him there had descended a peculiar hush. It was as if the mound itself was holding its breath…

His face still pressed to the earth, Phoenix opened his eyes.

It was a moment before he realized that he was staring straight down into one of the narrow little hollows ... and that it was quite, quite empty.

He lifted his head, then caught his breath.

To one side of the empty hollow, wreathed in dust, was a shadowy figure.

It seemed that someone had been waiting for him.

14.
THE REWARD

It was a face he knew almost as well as his own — a face that had stared out at him countless times from the faded old family album.

Younger than the one he was used to, it was true. Much younger. But very definitely the same.

Still gripping the anchored bolt, Phoenix swallowed back the dryness in his throat.

"Is it really you?" he whispered.

The ghostly figure looked back at him sadly.

For a time there was silence, except for the churning of the pit in the centre of the mound.

"You've been watching me, haven't you?" said Phoenix. "You were here earlier on."

He frowned.

"But why do you look so sad? I don't understand.

You must realize now that what happened to Lorenzo wasn't your fault?"

The figure bowed its head.

"But it wasn't!" cried Phoenix. "Really, it wasn't!"

He winced as the bolt pulsed with a fresh surge of heat.

Very soon he was going to have to put it back inside the empty hollow. There was no way this lull in the tremors was going to last for long. And once the bolt had been replaced, who knew whether this sad-looking child-ghost of his mother would still be here for him to talk to? But he had a few moments, surely? Enough time at least to try and convince her that she wasn't to blame for everything that had happened all those years ago. And until then he mustn't let go of the bolt, however much it hurt. It was the only thing standing between him and the menacing pit beyond.

"Look," he went on. "I don't know exactly what went on that day – whether you could have stopped Lorenzo from coming over here or not. But you weren't to know the mound was cursed. That there was something – some*one* – down there, protecting their treasure. You saw what happened to me, didn't you? And you must have heard what I told Rose? About the voice luring me into the river?"

He shuddered.

"Nothing could have prevented me from obeying that voice. Nothing in the world. And it must have been the same for poor Lorenzo. He wouldn't have had any choice."

His mother's ghost looked back at him – and there was a new stillness in her face.

"It's why you're here on the mound, isn't it?" said Phoenix. "Because you've never been able to let go of what happened?"

He shook his head.

"You've got to put it all behind you now. *Whatever* that might mean for you. Somehow you've got to move on to something better."

A smile flickered on his lips.

"Just listen to me!" he said. "Lecturing my own mother! It's kind of hard to know what to say to you."

He glanced away.

"Except – well, except there is something I want to say. I want you to know how much I've missed you. You were such a brilliant mum to me – the best anyone could ever wish for. And it's really hard without you. But I've got to get on with it. I've got to pull myself together and try to enjoy life."

The ghostly figure reached towards him, and for the briefest of seconds Phoenix felt the whisper of a touch upon his shoulder.

"You know I lost the little silver angel, don't you?" he murmured. "It was his, wasn't it? It belonged to Lorenzo."

The figure smiled.

"Then I'm doubly sorry for losing it. I know what that angel must have meant to you, and I wish more than anything else that I could have it back."

They both started as a familiar rumbling rose up from the depths of the earth.

"Looks like someone's losing patience," murmured Phoenix, biting his lip as the iron bolt seared into his fist.

He stared at his mother's ghost.

"I'll never forget you," he said. "Never. And I hope you get to be with him again. With Lorenzo, I mean."

He wrenched the bolt from the ground and unclenched his blistering fingers over the empty hollow, watching as it dropped into place.

The rumbling died to nothing – and looking up, he saw that the dust was melting away … the milky light was fading … the vortex was slowing … the hollows and the central pit were filling in…

A shower of earth jetted up from the middle of the mound, as if in some final gesture of farewell, landing on the surface with a gentle patter – and then there was only stillness and silence.

Phoenix turned back towards the place where the

ghostly figure had been.

But he knew even before he looked that it had vanished.

Rose watched as the veil of dust and sleet dissolved and a golden brightness filtered through the air.

Something quite remarkable had happened up there, that much was obvious. Something which seemed to have quelled the warrior-king's anger.

The gulf in the earth was sealing itself back up, and as the sun scorched away the damp coldness she could feel her fears for Phoenix melting away too.

He'd only been gone five or ten minutes, yet it felt like hours since he had scrambled up the side of the mound, and with each fresh tremor her view had become more and more obscured. She hadn't been able to hear much either, except for the juddering of the earth and the howling of the wind, although in the last few minutes she could have sworn she had heard the sound of her cousin's voice.

She waited until the chasm had mended completely – and then, still holding the toy boat, she began to clamber up the mound.

She saw him at once, standing to one side, his back towards her.

Everything had changed: the ground was smooth

and flat and the outline of the boat had disappeared beneath a covering of fresh new grass. All that remained of what had been was a light scattering of soil in the centre of the mound.

Rose approached her cousin, her footfall soft upon the grass, and laid a hand on his shoulder.

He spun round. "Rose!" he gasped. He stared at her, his face chalky-white. "I … I thought you were someone else. I thought…"

"You thought what?" said Rose. "It was only ever going to be me, wasn't it?"

"Yes … yes … of course… Ignore me. I…"

Rose's expression softened.

"You thought it was that silhouette, didn't you?" she said. She squeezed his shoulder. "I honestly don't think you'll be seeing that again, Phoenix. It's all over now. Whatever miracle you've managed to work up here, everything's gone back to normal."

Phoenix bent his head.

"You're right," he said. "I won't be seeing it again."

He sank down to the ground.

"The trouble is, part of me wishes I still could. Part of me wishes it was here this minute, scaring the living daylights out of me like before."

"But—"

"It was my mother, Rose. She was the silhouette.

She'd been watching me from the moment I set foot on here."

"Your *mother*?"

Phoenix sighed.

"I came back to have one more look at the treasure," he said. "I couldn't help myself. But then the mound went crazy and I suddenly realized what I had to do. I needed to return the last iron bolt."

He looked up at his cousin.

"The pit started to suck me towards it and I was almost dragged in. But I managed to get myself back, and just as I'd found the empty hollow and was about to drop the bolt inside, I saw her. The child-ghost of my mother. Exactly as she had been when she lived here."

Rose stared back at him, open-mouthed.

"She'd obviously spent her entire life believing she was to blame for Lorenzo's death," went on Phoenix. "That's why she ended up here when she died, unable to rest in peace."

He reached out in front of him and broke off a blade of grass.

"Of course, when she saw what happened to me, she must have realized the same thing had happened to Lorenzo. But I think she needed my blessing too. It was as if she needed to hear it from me that it hadn't been her fault – that most of what had taken place that day had been beyond her control."

He held the grass taut between his fingers, then snapped it in two.

"I was only with her for a few minutes and then the rumbling started up again and I had to put the bolt back into the earth. And … and when I turned round she'd gone."

There was a long silence, broken only by the cry of a solitary curlew circling above them.

"I know what you're thinking," said Phoenix at last. "You reckon I dreamed up the bit about my mother, don't you? You reckon it's just what I *want* to believe."

Rose sat down beside him.

"I don't think that at all," she said. "I believe what you say completely. Why shouldn't I?"

She turned Lorenzo's toy boat round in her hands.

"If you really want to know, I think you're pretty cool. To have worked it all out like that. And to have made everything all right again."

Phoenix flushed.

He shot his cousin a quick grin. "You're just about OK, you know. For a girl, that is."

Rose lunged at him, and the little boat jerked out of her hands and landed on the ground between them.

"What are you going to do with that, then?" she said, gesturing towards it. "Will you take it home with you?"

Phoenix shook his head.

"No," he said. "I reckon it belongs here at Gravenhunger."

He picked up the boat and ran his finger over the sweep of the hull.

"I guess Lorenzo never did get to sail it that day, did he? Perhaps we should do the job for him and let it go on the river. What do you think?"

Rose smiled. "I think it's exactly what he would've wanted."

"Then let's do it," said Phoenix, pulling himself upright.

He turned and started to walk towards the edge of the mound.

"Hang on a minute," said Rose, halfway to her feet. "Phoenix, wait! What's that over there in the middle?"

Phoenix looked at where she was pointing.

"It's just a bit of earth, that's all. The pit had a sort of crazy last-minute fit and chucked up a load of loose soil…"

He trailed off as a brilliant ray of sunlight illuminated something small and bright lying in amongst the scattered earth.

The next moment he was darting forward.

"The silver angel!" he cried, scooping it up. "How did that get there? It's like it's been given back to me."

He pressed his mother's keepsake into his hand. "It was Lorenzo's, you know. At least, I think that's what my mother was telling me. It feels as if I've got a bit of both of them now."

He rejoined his cousin and together they made their way down the side of the mound, basking in the welcome heat of the sunshine.

When they reached the riverbank, Phoenix knelt down and settled Lorenzo's boat on the water.

"There," he said, giving it a gentle nudge. "Go, little boat. Go where you belong."

They watched as it bobbed away down the sparkling river, heading for the open sea.

"Time to get back," said Phoenix, making for the tree-trunk bridge. "You never know, Dad might change his mind about leaving when he sees what's happened to the weather."

Rose glanced at him. "Is that what you want? To stay?"

Her cousin nodded.

"Just so long as we don't go messing about on the mound, I reckon we could have a great time here this summer."

They shuffled across the bridge and set off through the forest, pausing as they heard an engine purring down the track towards them.

"It's Dad!" cried Phoenix. "Come on! I'll race you!"

He charged onward, shielding his eyes against the flashes of sunlight streaming between the trees.

Bursting out of the pines into the stillness of the hot July afternoon, he let out a low cry.

From the branches of the old apple tree, the two wooden swings hung as they had always done.

But they were no longer still.

They were moving together in perfect harmony, backwards and forwards … backwards and forwards…

And above the noise of the approaching engine, Phoenix and Rose could hear the unmistakable sound of faraway laughter.

Also from
Harriet Goodwin…

THE HEX FACTOR

Xanthe Fox can't wait to turn thirteen, but as the
big day arrives her world starts to fall apart. Set-up
at school for something she didn't do, it seems her
age-old enemy, Kelly, is making trouble for her …
and as things escalate, even her best friend Saul
starts to doubt her innocence.

With the school threatening to expel her, and
mysterious glowing Xs appearing in front of her
eyes, Xanthe turns to Grandma Alice for help.
But what the old lady tells her will change
Xanthe's life for ever…

THE
HEX
FACTOR

Harriet Goodwin

THE HEX FACTOR
Dark Tide

Xanthe Fox has survived her first test as a
teenage True Witch, and defeated her Hexing
Witch enemy Donna – for now. Desperate to
learn all she can from Grandma Alice, Xanthe
spends all her free time at her house, much to
the grief of Saul, who's finally plucked up the
courage to ask her out.

Soon Xanthe is seeing bright, glowing Xs,
which are getting more powerful by the
day. Convinced that a bigger hex than ever
is being sparked, Xanthe knows that she
must act – with or without the help of
the other True Witches…

Harriet Goodwin

THE HEX
FACTOR

Dark Tide

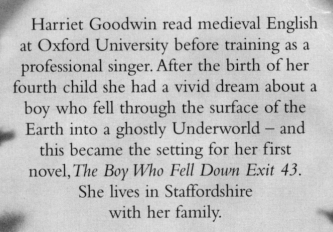

Harriet Goodwin read medieval English
at Oxford University before training as a
professional singer. After the birth of her
fourth child she had a vivid dream about a
boy who fell through the surface of the
Earth into a ghostly Underworld – and
this became the setting for her first
novel, *The Boy Who Fell Down Exit 43*.
She lives in Staffordshire
with her family.

**For more
about the author,
visit her website:**

www.harrietgoodwinbooks.com